ZANE PRESENTS

W9-BDH-170

THE
TRUTH
IS IN
THE WINE

A NOVEL

Dear Reader:

Everyone knows that when alcohol goes in, the truth usually comes out. In his latest novel, *The Truth Is In The Wine*, *Essence* bestselling author, Curtis Bunn, puts that theory to task. When a couple struggling to decide whether to remain married or not decides to take their dream vacation to the Napa Valley in California, along with both of their mothers who cannot stand to breathe the same air, anything is likely to happen…and it does.

Happiness and pain in a marriage are often interchangeable and when two people truly love each other, things can change in the blink of an eye…or a roll in the hay. This novel could be a much-needed therapeutic aide for a lot of couples trying to make a decision about whether to stick it out with each other or part ways. It is an intense at times, humorous at times, portrayal of why family and love trump everything else. I am sure that readers will be engaged in the characters and story-line from the first page. Bunn is a prolific author who never tells the same story twice, a godsend in today's literary climate.

As always, thanks for supporting the authors of Strebor Books. We always try to bring you groundbreaking, innovative stories that will entertain and enlighten. I can be located at www.facebook.com/AuthorZane or reached via email at Zane@eroticanoir.com.

Blessings,

Zane

Publisher
Strebor Books International
www.simonandschuster.com/streborbooks

ZANE PRESENTS

THE
TRUTH
IS IN
THE WINE

A NOVEL

CURTIS BUNN

SBI

STREBOR BOOKS

NEW YORK LONDON TORONTO SYDNEY

Strebor Books
P.O. Box 6505
Largo, MD 20792
http://www.streborbooks.com

ISBN 978-1-59309-504-8
ISBN 978-1-4767-1146-1 (e-book)
LCCN 2013933667

First Strebor Books trade paperback edition October 2013

Cover design: www.mariondesigns.com
Cover photograph: © Keith Saunders/Keith Saunders Photos

10 9 8 7 6 5 4 3 2 1

Manufactured in the United States of America

For information regarding special discounts for bulk purchases,
please contact Simon & Schuster Special Sales at 1-866-506-1949
or business@simonandschuster.com

The Simon & Schuster Speakers Bureau can bring authors to your
live event. For more information or to book an event, contact the
Simon & Schuster Speakers Bureau at 1-866-248-3049 or visit our
website at www.simonspeakers.com.

For my Felita, who is sweeter than any wine.
And that's the truth.

ACKNOWLEDGMENTS

Always, I give honor and praise to God for his unlimited blessings. He certainly carried me through this book. Thank you, Lord.

My family, which I love so much, remains to the core: my late father, Edward Earl Bunn, Sr.; he was not much of a wine-drinker, as I recall. Scotch was his drink of choice; my mother, Julia Bunn, who is simply wonderful; my brothers, Billy and Eddie and my sister, Tammy. My grandmother, Nettie Royster, remains our spiritual foundation.

Curtis, Jr. and Gwendolyn (Bunny) are my children, my life-blood, my heartbeats. My nephew, Gordon, has always been like a second son. And my niece, Tamayah (Bink Bink) and nephew Eddie, Jr. are blessings that I love so much. My cousins, Greg Agnew and Warren Eggleston, are like my brothers, as well as my brother-in-law, Deryk. And I am grateful for cousin Carolyn Keener and uncle Al and aunts Thelma and Barbara and Ms. Brenda Brown, who has been like an aunt/second mom much of my life.

Additionally, my wife Felita is my foundation, heart

and soul, super-duper closest friend and beacon of hope.

Again, Zane, Charmaine Roberts Parker and the entire Strebor Books/Atria/Simon & Schuster family have been great, and I am eternally grateful for you. I'm proud to be a part of the wonderful, talented Strebor family.

I enjoy listing by name the supporters because you all mean so much to me: My ace, Trevor Nigel Lawrence, Keith (Blind) Gibson, Kerry Muldrow, Randy Brown, Sam Myers, Ronnie Bagley, Tony Starks, Darryl Washington, Darryl (DJ) Johnson, Lyle Harris, Monya Bunch, Tony (Kilroy) Hall, Marc Davenport, Tami Rice-Mitchell, Brad Corbin, William Mitchell, J.B. Hill, Bob White, Kent Davis, Wayne Ferguson, Tony & Erika Sisco, Betty Roby, Kathy Brown, Venus Chapman, Nicole McDowell, Tara Ford, Flecia Brown, Christine Beatty, Greg Willis, Al Whitney, Brian White, Ronnie Akers, Jacques Walden, Dennis Wade, Julian Jackson, Mark Webb, Kelvin Lloyd, Frank Nelson, Hayward Horton, Mark Bartlett, Marvin Burch, Derrick (Nick Lambert), Gerald Mason, Charles E. Johnson, Harry Sykes, Kim Mosley, Ed (Bat) Lewis, Shelia Harrison, David A. Brown, Leslie LeGrande, Rev. Hank Davis, Susan Davis-Wigenton, Donna Richardson, Sheila Wilson, Curtis West, Bruce Lee, Val Guilford, Derek T. Dingle, Ramona Palmer, Joi Edwards, Warren Jones, Deberah (Sparkle) Williams, Leon H. Carter, Zack Withers, Kevin Davis, Sybil & Leroy Savage, Avis Easley, Demetress Graves, Anna Burch, Natalie Crawford, Najah Aziz,

George Hughes, Monica Harris Wade, Yetta Gipson, Mary Knatt, Serena Knight, Sonya Perry, Denise Taylor, Diana Joseph, Derrick (Tinee) Muldrow, Rick Eley, Marty McNeal, D.L. Cummings, Rob Parker, Cliff Brown, D. Orlando Ledbetter, Garry Howard, Stephen A. Smith, Clifford Benton, Len Burnett, Lesley Hanesworth, Sherline Tavenier, Jeri Byrom, E. Franklin Dudley, Skip Grimes, Carla Griffin, Jeff Stevenson, Angela Norwood, Lateefah Aziz, Billy Robinson, Jay Nichols, Ralph Howard, Paul Spencer, Jai Wilson, Garry Raines, Glen Robinson, Dwayne Gray, Jessica Ferguson, Carolyn Glover, David R. Squires, Kim Royster, Keela Starr, Mike Dean, Veda McNeal, Dexter Santos, John Hughes, Mark Lassiter, Tony Carter, Kimberly Frelow, Michele Ship, Michelle Lemon, Zain, Tammy Thompson, Karen Shepherd, Carmen Carter, Erin Sherrod, Tawana Turner-Green, Sheryl Williams-Jones, Vonda Henderson, Danny Anderson, Keisha Hutchinson, Olivia Alston, John Hollis, Dorothy (Dot) Harrell, Aggie Nteta, LaKesha Williams, Ursula Renee, Carrie Haley, Anita Wilson, Tim Lewis, Sandra Velazquez, Patricia Hale, Pam Cooper, Michelle Hixon, Regina Troy, Denise Thomas, Andre Aldridge, Brenda O'Bryant, Ron Thomas, Pargeet Wright, Laurie Hunt, Deborah Sharpe, Mike Christian, Sid Tutani, Tracie Andrews, Toni Tyrell, Tanecia Raphael, Tammy Grier, Roland Louis, April Tarver, Penny Payne, Cynthia Fields, TaToya Tokley, Dr. Yvonne Sanders-Butler, Alicia Guice, Clara LeRoy, Denise Bethea, Hadjii

Hand, Petey Franklin, Sibyl Johnson, Shauna Tisdale and The Osagyefuo Amoatia Ofori Panin, King of Akyem Abuakwa, Eastern Region of Ghana, West Africa.

Special thanks and love to my great alma mater, Norfolk State University (Class of 1983); the brothers of Alpha Phi Alpha (especially the Notorious E Pi of Norfolk State); Ballou High School (Class of '79), ALL of Washington, D.C., especially Southeast and the team at www.atlanta blackstar.com.

I am also grateful to all the readers and book clubs that have supported my work over the years and to my many literary friends Nathan McCall, Carol Mackey, Linda Duggins, Terrie Williams, Kimberla Lawson Roby, Walter Mosley.

I'm sure I left off some names; I ask your forgiveness. If you know me you know it is an error of the head, not the heart. :-) I appreciate and I am grateful for you.

Peace and blessings,
CURTIS

In vino veritas (in vee-noh ver-i-tas) *Latin*.
In wine, there is truth. A Latin expression that
suggests people are more likely to say what they
really feel under the influence of alcohol.

CHAPTER 1
CONFLICTING EMOTIONS

The pain shot up Ginger Wall's left arm, a jolt that rendered half of her body immobile. Her heartbeat was rapid, even though it felt like her chest was collapsing. Breathing was a chore. She was sure she was going to die.

No one was around to help her. No one was around because there was no one in her life. Her husband was her husband, but pretty much in name only; their marriage was on a spectacular descent. And he was in the house, anyway. Her daughter, whom she had smothered like a blanket, was just off to college. The few friends she maintained were kept at a distance. She was alone, and that thought pushed her to the edge of death.

Unable to move and desperate for air, Ginger resigned herself to dying—right there behind the wheel of her Lexus coupe in the garage of her modest townhouse near downtown Atlanta.

Seconds went by, then minutes, and finally she passed out. When she came to a few minutes later, the pain was gone. She could breathe easily. There was relief of the pressure she felt on her chest.

It almost seemed like a dream, like she pulled into the garage and passed out from exhaustion, and that scary moment came to her in her sleep. The reality was that the thought of entering a loveless house paralyzed her with anxiety and fear. She knew it was not a dream because her face was damp with tears.

Ginger had recently returned from dropping off her only child, Helena, at college. Paul, her husband, said his goodbyes to his baby girl at the airport, a fear of flying keeping him from making the trip to Washington, D.C.

But not her mom. Helena had become Ginger's everything. Right around the time Paul was laid off from his job as a heating and air conditioning repair specialist was when their marriage turned into an eighteen-wheeler going downhill with no brakes. He lost his self-esteem and she, eventually, lost interest. The combination made for a mundane existence and rapid fall over an eleven-month period.

This was not easy to accept for Ginger. She was crushed, crestfallen. It was if someone had died. As if *she* had died.

Only she hadn't. She was alive, but not living. To breathe, Ginger threw what was left of herself into Helena, serving as mother, chef, security, fan, chauffeur and anything else that kept her occupied and gave her some sense of fulfillment. That was why she pleaded with her child to attend a local college; her going away was akin to pulling the plug on the activity in Ginger's life.

"Mom, you know I love you and I'm going to miss you," Helena said when she decided to attend college in Washington, D.C. "But I've got to get away. Not from you, but from Atlanta. You are the one who told me when I turned fifteen that I should go to school out of town, that it would help me to grow up and be responsible. Ever since then that has been my goal. Plus, you have Dad."

Somehow, through the strife, they managed to shield Helena, to, indeed, fool her. She thought her parents were in a fulfilling relationship. If she had taken the time to *really* pay attention, she would have noticed that all the cheery conversation around the house was between her and her mom or her and her dad. There was only token dialogue between her parents, and none of it loving.

But she was merely seventeen when the downturn began; *her* life was the focal point of *her* existence. She simply did not notice.

One night while Helena was at a school play, the troubles in the marriage reached a crescendo.

"I thought about it. I thought about it a lot," Paul said, rising from the dinner table with Ginger. "I've got to go."

Ginger had a forkful of risotto headed toward her mouth when he said that. She dropped it into her plate below. He said it so casually, as one would reveal it was raining outside. The words registered with Ginger instantly, but for a nanosecond, though, she thought he meant he had to leave the dining room because there was a game on television he had to see. Or that he was tired and needed to go to bed early. Or that he wanted something from the store and had to go and get it. It could *not* have meant what it really sounded like he meant. It was not what he said; it was the *way* he said it that clued her in.

So, she did what anyone would do: She asked for confirmation. "What do you mean?"

Paul continued toward the kitchen. He did not bother to turn around.

"Divorce, Ginger," he said, again so nonchalantly that it was staggering. "Divorce."

Ginger reached for her glass of homemade tea and knocked it over, spilling its contents across the table and onto the hardwood floor. She was frozen there, unable to move until her emotions switched from confusion to anger. It was not April Fool's Day and Paul was not a joking kind of man. He, in fact, had become so serious, that Ginger and Helena privately called him "Heart Attack," as in "Serious as a heart attack."

Her anger allowed her to rise from the table and storm her way to the kitchen, where Paul was uncorking a second bottle of Malbec from the vast collection of wines he coveted like rare coins. He did not share the first bottle with his wife.

Ginger was five-foot-six, but appeared smaller when side-by-side with Paul, who was eight inches taller.

Looking up at him, she demanded: "What are you talking about, Paul?"

Ginger raised her voice when her husband did not answer. "Paul, what the hell are you talking about?"

"Don't act like this is some surprise," he said, finally. There was an edge to his voice—and a coldness, too. "This has been building for a while now. I'm fifty years old. You're only forty-seven. And—"

"Are you drunk? I'm forty-three," Ginger interrupted.

"No, I'm not drunk. And, okay, you're forty-three," Paul went on. "Anyway, we have some time to live still. Face it: We're not good together anymore."

"And this is the result?" Ginger asked. "You making a decision for both of us? No discussion about it? No counseling? Nothing? And what about our daughter, Paul? What about her?"

"Helena is a smart girl and she's strong," he said. "She will adjust. She'll be fine."

Ginger was not so sure about that. She and her daughter were close, but she was a daddy's girl. This news would rock her.

"Well, you tell her why you're breaking up this family," Ginger said. "You tell her that she and I are not good enough for you."

"This is not about Helena," Paul said, and a chill ran through Ginger's body despite how heated she was.

"So, it's about me? You don't want *me* anymore?" she asked. It was a rhetorical question because she knew the answer. But Paul answered anyway.

"I'm simply not sure about this marriage anymore," he said. He sipped his wine. "I'm sorry. I really am. I can't make you happy. And you don't try to make me happy. We've had sex one time in the last nine months. One time, a few weeks ago. And that was because we both were drunk.

"So why should we stay in a marriage for appearance sake? Or even for Helena? It wouldn't be teaching her the right thing."

"And it's teaching her the right thing by breaking up her family?" Ginger asked. She wanted to continue, but it suddenly hit her that going back and forth with Paul would give him the impression she was trying to convince him to stay, which she did not want to do. No doubt, she was devastated and hurt; she had built her life around her family. But she was prideful, too, and somewhere in their back-and-forth she decided, "Fuck him."

"I only ask that you do two things for me," she said. "Pick up your daughter from school and explain this to her."

"I will talk to Helena," Paul said. "But not tonight."

"You bastard," Ginger fired back. "You had it all planned out, huh? So who's your woman? Who's your side chick?"

Paul studied his wife, scanned her from head-to-toe and back again. There was a time looking at her smooth skin and full, pouty lips and dark eyes would mesmerize him. Not anymore. He held animus toward her that he did not bother to explain.

"Believe it or not," he said as calmly as one would give driving directions, "it's not about being with someone else. It's about being away from you."

And as tranquil as Paul was, Ginger turned equally irate. "I have done nothing but love you and be here for you and provide a nice home for you," she said. "You're such an egomaniac to try to belittle me. That's very hateful of you. But it shows you don't deserve me. You have been depressed since losing your job and I have been supportive and encouraging. Since we're being honest about everything, let me tell you this: You're a selfish pig. All you've ever thought about was yourself. You never considered how hard this whole thing has been for me. And that makes you a selfish pig.

"I'm woman enough to admit that I'm hurt by all of this. But the more I talk the more strength I get. I don't mean to call you names, but you're a loser. And whatever God has in store for you, well, good luck with that because He does not reward selfish pigs."

"Yeah, that's really mature, Ginger," Paul said. "You wishing bad on me. I won't stoop that low."

"You'd have to cut off your legs to get any lower than you are," Ginger said.

"I could say something, but I'm not going to," Paul responded. "But I will say this: You call being a nasty, mean, cold person supportive of me? That's all you have been. And that's not supportive."

Paul looked at Ginger with a strange expression. "I'm going to pick up Helena," he said. "I'll explain everything to her, but not now. She's happy. I will, though, in due time."

"Yeah, right," Ginger said. "You'll explain what you want to explain—not the truth, I'm sure."

Paul finished his wine, corked the bottle and placed it in its proper place among the alphabetized collection. He looked at his wife, who could not detect the pain that engulfed him. He hid it well, but inside he cried. Finally, before tears seeped from his eyes, he turned and walked away.

Ginger was left standing there to struggle with an influx of emotions that came crashing down. She waited until she heard the garage close, indicating Paul had gone.

It was then that she was overcome with a confluence of pain, shock, hurt, disappointment and failure. She cried. She laughed. She perspired—all over a three- or four-minute span. Ginger thought she was having a breakdown. "I'm OK," she said aloud. "I'm OK."

But she wasn't.

CHAPTER 2
SAVING GRACE

As Ginger sat in the garage that evening, fearful that she was dying, Paul stood in the house, perhaps fifty feet away, feeling as alive as ever, as if he were starting a new life. His hands shook, but not from some kind of breakdown. It was from the possibilities, from relief, from joy, from amazement. While his wife fretted coming into the loveless house she shared with a man who wanted out, Paul held in his unsteady possession a lottery ticket that represented $8 million.

A whole new world was now his, one that suddenly had boundless possibilities.

Processing it all jolted him. He played the Georgia State Lottery because it seemed the thing to do. "You have to play to win," its slogan said. And yet he never expected to actually have the prized numbers.

In one sense, it was liberating: financial concerns, concerns that overwhelmed him and robbed him of his dignity, no longer existed. In another sense, there was trepidation: What to do? Where to begin? And in still another way there was a true dilemma: What to do about his wife?

He had $4 million or so coming to him after taxes, but it was not enough to bring him total joy. The reality was that he still loved Ginger. Yes, he told her he wanted out of the marriage, but he did not mean it. Not really. He was frustrated, almost depressed and did not see any other way to spare *her* life.

He wanted her love, *needed* her love. Before he lost his job, Paul was devoted and loving. He was not the most light-hearted guy, but Ginger could rely on him to love her and be there for her and their daughter. Losing his job changed him. He became distant and evil. His self-esteem evaporated. He felt no sense of self-worth. His changed disposition led to a troubled marriage.

Winning the money instantly turned Paul into the Paul of old. He felt totally rejuvenated. But he needed Ginger's love. Other than Diana, his high-school girlfriend, Ginger was the only woman he loved. And he wanted her love back. But he wanted her back on genuine terms; not because he became a millionaire.

After his outburst a few weeks earlier, when he told her he wanted a divorce, their "marriage" really leveled off. They spoke pleasantly enough to each other around their daughter, but that was it. Ginger gathered herself and displayed a lack of interest in Paul, a disregard for their marriage and a disinterest in trying to save it.

Paul was troubled. He had no idea he would get a financial windfall. When he did, still feeling like his life was incomplete told him something significant: He needed

Ginger. Buying back her love was akin to prostitution, and Paul viewed prostitution as an act against God.

Rather, he wanted to earn his wife's love and admiration, something he once possessed. The early years of their eighteen-year marriage were idyllic. It was a union that was nearly storybook in their joy and commitment to each other. When they learned they could not conceive a child, they adopted Helena, who was eight days old at the time. He was thirty-three and she was twenty-six, and having their daughter brought Paul and Ginger even closer, as they threw their love into making the child feel loved. And she did.

They did not have a lot of money but they had love and two salaries and they made it work—right up until around the time Paul was laid off his job. Over that nearly year of unemployment, his self-esteem plummeted like the economy and his weight increased by about fifteen unflattering pounds, all seemingly in his midsection and face.

Their marriage was not on the rocks; it was *under* the rocks. The getaway road trips to Miami and New Orleans ceased. The affection they showed each other—affection that at one time made other couples uncomfortable and envious at the same time—vanished like the rabbit in the magician's hat.

In the month after he told Ginger he wanted a divorce, they only seemed to tolerate each other while uttering nary a loving word between them. Paul was mum because he was depressed and she was displeased because her man no longer was the provider and comforter he had been. And he blamed her for his woes.

Her displeasure manifested itself in more and more time away with Helena and away from Paul—anything to not be around her husband whose manhood was assaulted with unemployment.

But Paul loved his wife and he believed she still loved him. At least, he wanted to believe that. Circumstances got in the way, he told himself. Looking down at that lottery ticket shaking in his hand, he believed he had the elixir to their toxic union.

The fix was not directly in how the money would influence his wife, however. It was in how it would impact *him*. The swagger, confidence, self-assuredness returned, and so he was immediately extracted from the doldrums. His renewed vim and vigor would be the keys to Ginger feeling better about him and, consequently, rescuing their marriage. That was his hope.

However, to make sure she would return to the loving woman he admired for the right reasons, he almost immediately determined he could not tell her of his winnings. Surely she would at least act as if she were back on board knowing the new extent of his bank account. If she was coming back, he wanted it to be on his merits, not his luck.

As his wife, she was entitled to half of the jackpot. He was not trying to avoid giving it to her—$2 million surely would be enough to live a cherished life, he reasoned. But he really needed to see if he could repair the damage that wrecked their marriage and restore the love from Ginger he used as fuel.

His shaking stopped as he worked his brain to conjure up something he could tell her that would at least minimize the questions of his sudden fat pockets.

Paul could claim the money at any time, but decided he would wait a few weeks. He wanted the attention around the drawing to diminish before he contacted the lottery office. Paul liked to play the numbers, but Ginger berated him about doing so, saying, "That's an ignorant way to waste money."

But Paul continued to play, only he did so in silence; Ginger had no idea. And neither she nor anyone knew about his winning numbers. He had no formula. There were no birthdays or license plate numbers or addresses. He selected random numbers that popped into his head for no particular reason.

Of all the things that could have been overwhelming his brain—where to travel, what to buy, how to celebrate, never having to work again—Paul's thoughts centered on saving his marriage. He considered Ginger his "whole-mate," saying "You make me whole" in reciting his vows at their wedding. Ginger was it for him, from the first time they met at the quaint bar at Aria restaurant in the Buckhead section of Atlanta.

Ginger was with friends celebrating a birthday. When

she went to the bar to order a bottle of wine, Paul—after observing her alluring presence—volunteered his expertise.

"That bottle of wine you ordered will have the effect you want; it will get you drunk," he said, smiling. "But if you want to have a great-tasting wine that also will get you where you want to get, I would recommend this."

He pointed to a sixty-five-dollar bottle of Palmeri Riesling. Ginger took his advice and later came back to thank him for the suggestion. She loved it. Paul was happy she came back to the bar, where he sat alone, sipping wine.

"You should let me be your sommelier," he said.

"Maybe I would if I knew what that was," Ginger answered. "You might be trying to set me up."

They laughed. "A sommelier is basically a wine steward, someone who knows and understands wines and can recommend the right one for the right meal, right occasion, right mood," he said.

"OK, I get it," she answered. "And you'll be my personal sommelier? How did I get so lucky?"

"You obviously are a lucky person," he said with a no-nonsense look on his face. Then he smiled.

He had her then. Ginger was intrigued, soon in love and less than two years later they were married. And now Paul, in an instant, was an unlikely millionaire, married to a woman he loved despite having told her he wanted a divorce.

Because he was so down about himself, he did not know how to change the course of his marriage. If only he could get a job, it would do something toward his self-esteem and therefore bring out the person she fell in love with, instead of the person that became mired in so much self-pity.

Well, he came up better than finding a job. He hit the lottery, and his self-esteem rushed back to him as if injected into his bloodstream.

Paul did not have any siblings and was not sure when he would tell his mother, although he would take care of her in every way she desired. Alvin, meanwhile, was the ace among his plethora of friends, his Super Glue-tight "dog" of twenty-two years. When Paul got the trembling out of his system, he screamed so loudly his head hurt. Then he shed joyous tears. Then he called Alvin, whom he referred to as Big Al.

"Get over here right now. I don't care what you're doing; please, get here now," Paul said.

He alarmed Big Al. "What's wrong, boy? Talk to me."

"Can't. Not over the phone. Just get here," Paul said. "Big news."

"Twenty minutes," Big Al said.

The news was so big that Big Al could not contain his glee. He knew Paul being a millionaire meant he was one, too. His life as he knew it also had changed. That's how tight they were.

And so he leaped around Paul's as if on a pogo stick.

Paul sat there watching and laughing. He never let the ticket out of his hands.

"I'd rather not have her than have her back because I have money," Paul told Big Al.

"Why do you want her back at all?" Alvin shot back. "You know how I feel about Ginger. She's cool with me. But there's a new world out there for you. You can do anything you want and acquire anything you want. I mean, seriously. You're telling me you have four million dollars coming to you and you want to stay with a woman who has basically turned her back on you when stuff got tight? Let me tell you something: If I were *happily* married and hit the lottery for four mil, I'd get a divorce. Ain't nothing one woman could do for me with that kinda money."

"You would say that, Big Al," Paul said. "But then you don't have your 'wholemate.' I do. All you have are 'whore-mates.' It went bad for us, yeah. But now we can get it back."

"You think she won't get inspired to act like she's happy with all that money?" Big Al wanted to know.

"That's why I said I'm not telling her—at least not right now," Paul said. "I'm going to act like everything is the same."

"How can you have that money and act like everything is the same? Are you crazy?" Big Al said.

"Discipline," Paul answered. "This is important. This is my life. This is my wife. I recognize where her head is: she's disappointed that I'm not contributing to the household as I have, as I promised, as I'm supposed to. I told her a few weeks ago that I wanted a divorce. I didn't want to hold her back. So, I need to know where Gin's heart is. I haven't been able to find out before now because my head has been messed up. An out-of-work man is a man with a burden that only another out-of-work man can understand. I'm fifty years old. Been working since I was fourteen—that's thirty-six years straight where I earned a living.

"To be out of work for almost year took something out of me. I couldn't really convey it to her. I fell into a funk and she into a funk about me. I don't like it, but I can't blame her. I was supposed to be the man for her, to provide. Not working drained some of my manhood, in her eyes."

"It's not like you weren't trying to get employed," Big Al said. "Or that you quit your job. You got downsized. Millions of guys have been downsized. And since then you have been hitting the bricks, interviewing, trying to get on. It's a bad time in the country, no matter how hard President Obama tries. Seems like if you were trying to get work she would understand and not simply check out on you.

"But, hey, that's just me. Anyway, so what's your plan? Anyone else gets rich, they act like they just got rich. You... you're gonna act like nothing changed? I gotta see this."

"Well, not exactly," he said. "I was part of a major class action suit against a bank that was overcharging on overdraft fees for twenty years. Ginger knows about it. I'm gonna tell her I got a settlement check of five thousand for that and that my income tax check came from last year—a little more money.

"Then I'm going to take her on a trip we both said we really wanted to go on before I lost my job—to the Napa Valley in California, to the wine country. We never went because I don't like to fly. But I'm going to for this.

"Al, this is my chance to get my life back the way I want it, but even better because we'll have each other and no more financial issues. Truth be told, I don't want anyone else. I want Ginger."

"Well, good luck, my brother," Al said. "I gotta get home. But when you're ready to start really spending that money, hit me up."

"You know I got you, man," Paul said. "First thing to do is line up your bills. We're gonna pay all them off and go from there. I'll have some nice cash for you."

They shook hands and slapped each other on the back.

"Tomorrow!" Paul yelled to Al as he walked toward his car.

An hour later, after he had pinched himself and the reality of the money set it, he heard the garage door open, indicating Ginger was home. The timing for the money was ideal; they had wiped out their savings for their daughter's first year of college. Paying for her education no longer would be a worry.

It seemed his only worry was if his wife would embrace him trying to mend their broken marriage.

CHAPTER 3
PICKING UP
THE PIECES

Paul got concerned when he realized Ginger had been in the car about fifteen minutes after he heard the garage door go up. He went to the refrigerator and pulled out a bottle of Viognier and two glasses.

Before he could go check on Ginger, she emerged, moving slowly, with her head down. She was down about her daughter being off to college and scared about the panic attack she had.

"Hey," Paul said with a level of concern in his voice— something Ginger had not heard in some time, "You OK?"

Ginger was stunned by his concern. She had heard no caring inflection in his voice for months, not toward her, anyway. She lifted her head and looked at him. Paul looked different, she noticed right away. He stood more upright and his eyes were bright, not sullen.

"Do you care, Paul?" she said, walking past him to the living room, where she sat on the couch.

Paul did not answer. He went to the kitchen and retrieved the wine and the glasses. He placed it on the coffee table in front of Ginger. She was confused. He had not offered her any of his precious wine in months.

"Ginger," he said, "I do care."

"Since when?" she asked.

Paul poured wine into the glasses. He picked up one and handed it to Ginger. She looked at the glass for several seconds, looked at her husband and finally reached for the glass.

"I have always cared, Gin," he said. "I just…"

"You just what, Paul?"

"I just lost who I was," he said.

Ginger did not respond. She sat back on the couch, wine in hand.

Paul went on. "I want you to realize that I'm sorry."

"You said you want a divorce, Paul," she shot out.

"I know and I didn't mean it," he said.

"So why would you say something so hurtful?" Ginger said. "You said you wanted to get away from me. You think that didn't hurt me, hurt my feelings?"

"I didn't mean it," he said. "Listen, I was depressed. I was miserable. You won't believe this, but I thought I would be doing the right thing by letting you move on. I didn't see anything getting better and…I…I don't know where that came from—divorce—but I just said it."

"You don't just say you want a divorce, Paul," she said.

"I just said it," he responded. "I don't want a divorce, Gin. I want us to get back to where we used to be. I really do."

"Why? Why would you want that after how bad it has been?" she asked.

"Please taste your wine," Paul said. "It's good."

"Paul," Ginger said, exasperated.

"OK, I'm just saying," he said. He sipped his wine and added: "Anyway, think about it: Our baby is off to college. It's only you and me. This is the perfect time for us to find what we used to have."

Ginger finally tasted the wine. It was good—clean, light, fresh, floral.

"I don't know how to respond to this, Paul," she said. "I was in the car just now and I felt like I was dying. I dreaded coming in here and dealing with your attitude and total disregard for me. I literally was in the car crying. I couldn't breathe."

"What?"

"Yes, I'm serious," she said. "I felt like there was nothing for me to come into this house to, no love. So, for you to tell me you didn't mean all the awful things you said to me, the way you have treated me the last few weeks.... I don't know."

"You're supposed to be skeptical," Paul said. "I understand it. I'm not asking you to do anything except have an open mind. I want to work this thing out. It's very important to me."

Ginger took a big gulp of the wine, and it went straight to her head. She sipped more, and she could feel a change coming over her from it. When that happened, she became audacious.

"So, what's this about? You want sex?" she said. "All of a sudden you're serving me wine and you want to work it out? Look at you. You're all shaven and even have on cologne. What's going on? I don't get it. It was bad before, but the last three weeks have been terrible.

"And now you want to work it out? That's hard to believe. I don't care what you say."

Paul knew his wife and he knew that the wine was kicking in. He also knew that challenging her would result in her getting more and more combative, especially after she finished her glass and immediately poured herself another.

There were times when he would challenge her. But this was not one of them.

"You will see over time," he said. "Ginger, let's make this work."

"How do you propose we do this, Mr. I Want A Divorce?" she said.

Paul smiled.

"What's so funny?" she wanted to know. "You laughing at me?"

"No. I was thinking we should take a trip," he said.

"A trip?" Ginger cracked. "To where? Fantasy Island?"

"I was thinking the trip we have been talking about for years—to Napa Valley," Paul said.

"Napa? You want to drive across country?"

"No," he said. "Let's fly."

"You wanna fly?" Ginger said. "Now I'm sure something's up. You're the same man who two days ago would not fly to see your daughter off at college. Now, you wanna fly to California with me to the wine country? Nah, something's going on. What's going on?"

"I regret not flying with you and Helena to D.C.," Paul said. "I do. I don't like flying, but I should have made the trip anyway for my daughter. I regret that. But I will fly up there and fly back with her when she comes home for the first time. I have to do that for her.

"But in the meantime, I think we should go to Napa and enjoy the wine and see if we can't bring this marriage back together."

Ginger remained confused. The idea sounded good to her. No matter how bad things had gotten, Paul was still her husband and she silently prayed for their marriage to be saved.

But her rational mind would not push aside obvious questions.

"How we gonna pay for this?" she asked. "The mortgage is due and we barely got Helena into college. You think we should borrow money to go on a vacation? I know you're not saying that."

"I'm not saying that at all," Paul said, sipping the last of his wine. "Something happened today. I got a call about the class-action suit. I have some money coming to me next week: seven thousand dollars.

"We can pay the mortgage and still have more than enough to go out there. Not long. Maybe three days. Enough to hit some vineyards and talk and see where we really are."

"So you got some money coming in for the first time in almost a year and you want to spend it all?" Ginger asked. "What about saving some? Bills come around every month, you know? Or did you forget?"

Paul was insulted but he did not let it show. It was not easy for him to hold back, but he did.

"Let's not forget that I have been providing some money for the longest here," he said calmly. "I worked with Eric cutting grass. I drove a cab. I worked at Home Depot. Don't act like I sat around here and did nothing. I'm not gonna let you put that out there like you might believe it's true. I have tried."

"You did, Paul," she conceded. "I won't deny that. But—"

"There is no but, Gin," he jumped in. "I have been through hell this year. You don't know what it's like to work all of your life and then one day, out of the blue, someone tells you that you can't work anymore. You can't provide for your family.

"That's not a small thing, Gin. It hurt. It changed me. And now I have some money coming my way; I deserve to take a vacation. You do, too."

He ain't never lied, she thought to herself. Ginger was emotionally spent. Between her daughter being off to college and the drama Paul inflicted—and now his one hundred eighty degrees in attitude change—she thought she was in a bad dream. Going away with anyone would be an elixir to her doldrums. And to Napa Valley, the one place she and Paul talked about really wanting to visit?

"You really want me to go?" Ginger asked.

"Yes," he answered.

"Well, if you really do, then you'd do this one thing for me," she said.

"What's that?" Paul wanted to know.

"Take my mother with us," she said.

It was such an out-of-left-field request that Paul spat the wine in his mouth out onto the coffee table and a little on Ginger.

"Damn, Paul. That's disgusting," she said, using a napkin to wipe off her arm.

"I'm sorry," he said. "You surprised me with that."

Madeline Price, Ginger's mother, lost her husband of 34 years about ten months prior, to a heart attack. He was working in the yard of their small ranch home near downtown Decatur, near Atlanta, with his wife, who went inside to fetch them some lemonade. When Madeline got back, her husband was facedown in the rose bushes, dead.

Her grieving was enormous and understandable. Theirs was a marriage the antithesis of most.

"I actually didn't heard my parents argue or speak of arguing in their last twenty years together," Ginger said. "If they were hiding it, they hid it well. You have seen them together—they were happy, like a fairy tale.

"So, taking her with us to the Wine Country would be really great for her. It hasn't been that long since my dad passed and she's done nothing but stay in the house. She needs to get away."

"We need to get away, too, Ginger," Paul said. "We really need this time. You think we can have the same experience with your mother there?"

"My mother being there won't interfere with anything between us," she said.

Ginger never took her eyes off of her husband and he never blinked. They were locked in, which was an advantage to Ginger, and she knew it. Paul melted at his wife's eyes and her desires. At least he used to.

"OK," he said. "OK. We'll work it out. It'll be good."

Ginger got up from the couch and hugged Paul, a show of affection so rare that he closed his eyes as they embraced, so as to savor the moment.

Then he opened them suddenly and pulled away from Ginger.

"What if I invite my mom, too?" he said. "She and your mom can keep each other company, finally get to know each other and maybe even end up liking each other. And that would give us some space to do something by ourselves."

Ginger was surprised; their parents were not close. They were not friends. There was no obvious dislike, but there was obvious unspoken discord.

"You didn't get that much money and now you're looking to spend it all on one trip?" she said.

"You weren't concerned about money when you asked about bringing your mom," Paul said.

"That's not the point," Ginger shot back.

"No, actually, it's exactly the point," Paul said. "I want my mom to come and suddenly you're worried about the money I spend? Well, if your mom is going, my mom should, too. She needs to get away as much as any of us."

Paul's point made Ginger think—and soften her stance. She was at Brenda Wall's the day after she told her husband when he came home from a round of golf: "I'm sorry. I'm moving out. I don't want to be married anymore."

And by the next morning, most of her belongings were in her new apartment in downtown Atlanta. She was that decisive. It was such a shocking move that she did not even get emotional about it.

"You're right," Ginger said. "Your mom and my mom both need to go someplace like Napa and clear their heads. It will be good for them. When?"

"I was thinking in a few weeks or so," Paul said. "I want to research where we should stay, what vineyards to see and so on and so forth."

"Paul, I don't think we should tell them about the trip yet," Ginger said. "Right now, I am agreeing to it, but I'm still not one hundred percent. I don't know. A lot of stuff has happened and I can't say I'm really over it."

"I'm sure you're not over it," he responded. "But life is too short to not get over it. This is a start, Gin. You know you want to go. You talk about how much I love wine, but you love it, too. To go there would be awesome. Listen, I'm willing to get on an airplane to do it. That's telling you how much I think we should do this."

Ginger simply stared at him, so he went on.

"Think about it: We need this. Think of how pictur-esque it is, how peaceful. Think of the great wines we will have. Think of how close we all will become because of this."

She took a deep breath. Almost an hour before she was in her garage, thinking she was about to die. Now, she had an invitation to live out a dream. How could she pass it up? How could she accept it, coming from a man who made her feel so bad about herself?

"Let me think about it, Paul," she said. "But I don't know if I should go with you. There's a lot of water under the bridge."

"I understand," Paul said. "I understand. But we're going. This is too good an idea to pass up. And think about your mother and how much she needs this trip. In the meantime, I'm going to do some research."

CHAPTER 4
WHAT'S IN A NAME?

His mother named him Paul. She liked the name because it went nicely, she thought, with their last name, which was Wall. She especially liked that in The Bible, Paul was a man who faithfully spread the word of God throughout the nations.

Not that she was a religious zealot or anything. Simply, she believed in the power of God and she wanted her son to have a name that was at least associated with the Almighty.

And so, that made the nickname she gave her only child all the more perplexing.

"Vino," she called him.

Unlike most who picked up nicknames as kids that followed them through adulthood, Paul was labeled "Vino" when he was twenty-one—the legal age to drink alcohol. It was then that he became a wine lover of extraordinary measure.

After dropping out of college one year before graduation, he celebrated by going out alone for a drink. As he had not consumed an alcoholic beverage to that point, the bartender at the Capital Grille in Atlanta recommended he try a glass of Cabernet Sauvignon.

"Start slowly," the man said.

He poured Paul some in a wide-rimmed, elegant glass that felt like a delicate instrument. The bartender, Jimmy, explained that the circumference of the glass allowed the wine to breath.

Paul started to ask, "Why does wine need to breathe?" but thought better of it. Instead, he admired it for a while, analyzed it. It was deep and rich in color, like blood, only darker. He had seen someone in a movie smell wine and swish it around in a glass before tasting it, and so he did that. The bartender stood there watching, curious about his reaction.

"This is a small part of history—your first drink," he said.

He swished the wine around his mouth as one would Listerine, but not as violently. He closed his eyes and finally swallowed. When he opened his eyes, the bartender was staring and smiling.

"Well…," he said.

Paul's response shocked the man. He talked of the wine's texture and its "oaky taste" and "smoky smell."

"It has a floral sense to it, too. I taste something like berries or dark cherries. And it was clean. I thought it would be chilled. But if it were chilled I think the taste of it would be different, not as powerful."

Jimmy, the bartender, stared at him. "So you were lying to me, huh?" he finally asked.

"Lying? No," Paul answered. "About what?"

"Then how could you come up with that kind of

analysis? Someone who never had wine couldn't possibly figure all that out," Jimmy said. "Even if you were wrong, it would be outrageous to think someone with no experience drinking would be able to come up with anything close to those thoughts. *And* it's the right analysis."

"I don't know," Paul said.

"Well, that makes you some kind of wine genius because I don't hear people who claim they appreciate and love wine give that kind of insight."

Paul did not know what to think. But he finished off the glass and then another, savoring each sip as a death row inmate would a last meal.

That night, he took his mother out to dinner. He broke the news that he quit school. "I tried it and realized, finally, it wasn't for me, Ma," he said. "No need to waste another year doing something I don't want to do."

His mom was stunned...in a bad way. "I had more dreams for you than becoming a dropout," she said.

Unfazed, Paul told her: "That's not how I look at it. I understand how you see it, though. But I see it as me waking up so I can finally start doing what I want to do," he said.

She was afraid to even ask what that might be, so she didn't. Instead, she sought the waiter.

"I will have a big, tall glass of bourbon," she said. "I don't care what brand. Straight."

"No," Paul told the waiter. "We'll have two glasses of wine. Pinot Noir."

She looked at her son as he gave detailed instructions.

"Since when do you drink?" she said. "And how do you know about wine?"

"Since this afternoon," he said. "I don't know a lot, but I know I like wine…a lot."

The Pinot arrived and he raised his glass. "This, Ma, is to following your dreams," he said, and they tapped glasses.

His mom sucked hers down as if it was Gatorade and she was stranded in the Arizona desert.

Paul was appalled. "That's not how you drink wine," he said. He then explained that wine was to be "pampered and savored, nurtured and seduced. Hold the glass by the stem; if you hold it by the glass your body temperature will warm it up."

"What's going on with you?" she said. "I don't understand any of this."

"It's easy to understand," Paul started. "I have taken back over my life. I'm twenty-one and I'm going to figure out exactly what I want to do. But it's going to be something I really want to do. Not some job to make money. I want to be happy to go to work."

His mother did not bother to challenge that logic, although she argued that having a college degree was a pedigree that could only help in whatever he wanted to do. After all, she knew her son. Paul had a passion for golf and playing Scrabble and watching *Jeopardy* on television. He enjoyed card games, especially "I Declare War," and "Tonk." Brenda Wall did not see a career in any of that.

Paul convinced her to let him dream outside of *her* dreams and work toward whatever career he developed an interest. His mom relented, but she was surprised that her son went through years of searching—painting, cooking, furniture-making—before he settled in on something that really resonated with him: working on heaters and air conditioners.

"I love it because I get to work with my hands and I get to figure out a problem and solve it," Paul explained. "It's not glamorous, but it's needed and I actually enjoy it."

He went to technical school for two years to get certified and he was on his way.

So he was at a good place. He identified his life's work and his love for wine increased.

For nearly two decades he dreamed of a vacation in the United States' finest region for wine: Napa Valley in northern California. One thing or another—getting married, an Achilles injury, lack of money—prevented him from fulfilling that ambition.

And after losing his job, it seemed he might not fulfill his dream any time soon but the lottery changed all that.

They decided to do something totally different: to visit Napa Valley for Thanksgiving. It was Ginger's idea. She woke up one morning with the feeling that if she was going on the trip, she'd rather it be in the fall and for the holiday. She had always wanted a destination Thanksgiving where she did not have to cook and clean, where she could enjoy the food and sit back like everyone else.

Even when she went to her mom's for Thanksgiving

or to her mother-in-law's, she always was obligated to help with the food and clean up. She did not want to do that again, especially with so much drama swirling around her marriage.

Helena, their daughter, went to Columbia, Maryland for the holiday with her college roommate and her family. Paul and Ginger were not happy about it, but they liked her roommate and family and were really glad their daughter had gained a true friend. So, the adults took to the journey across country.

Traveling there was relatively uneventful, if you discount Paul's panic attack, Ginger's frustration with her mother, Brenda Wall's unhappiness with the passenger sitting next to her and Madeline Price's displeasure about her daughter questioning her drinking on the plane. Other than that, it was all smooth.

And it all started so well. All parties gathered at Paul and Ginger's at seven o'clock Thanksgiving morning; flights were cheaper leaving on the holiday. Although Paul clearly could afford it, he went with the program so as to not arouse suspicion.

Ginger prepared a light breakfast of muffins, turkey bacon and fruit. Paul surprised everyone by arranging for a limousine to take them to the airport. They enjoyed the early meal and the luxurious ride to the airport without incident. Paul chalked it up to the early-morning hour. *They must be sleepy*, he thought to himself about the ladies.

Ginger had rebuffed all but one of Paul's sexual advances after he won the money. They had consumed two bottles of Fairfield Viognier from South Africa while watching the Presidential returns on November 6th. And when Barack Obama was reelected, all inhibitions came tumbling down in the celebration and relief.

It was an intense session, one that reminded Ginger of their early days together and made her forget their recent troubled times. Paul believed that night signaled they were on their way back to something significant.

But the next morning, Ginger was lukewarm, almost distant. It was almost as if the night before had not happened. When Paul tried to kiss her before leaving to go to "work," she moved away.

"What's wrong?" he said.

"You think everything is all right because we slept together, Paul?" she answered. "That changes nothing. We have problems and they are serious."

Paul was dumbfounded, but not deterred. "I understand," he said. "There's no need to act like it didn't happen because it did. So let's build on it and not take away from it."

Ginger knew he was right but her pride and stubbornness would not allow her to fall all the way back into the marriage after he so severely hurt her. "People think that as long as the man doesn't cheat on you, it's OK," she told her closest friend, Serena, a sweet and honest woman.

"I know," Serena said, "Like he should get credit for doing something he's supposed to do anyway."

"Right," Ginger said. "I'm glad he didn't cheat; don't get me wrong. But you can really hurt someone with your words and attitude. Paul sat at our dining room table and told me he didn't want me anymore. And he acted like it. And I'm supposed to simply melt when he says he didn't mean it? I don't think so."

"You're right, Ginger," Serena told her. "But don't be so caught up in what he said then. You know him better than anyone. You should be able to determine if he's sincere or not. And I'm not saying run back into his arms. But he is your husband and you do love him. If you can put your marriage back together, why wouldn't you?"

Then she added: "Never let him forget his words that hurt you. Don't use them against him. But if he needs to be reminded that he disappointed you…"

"That's why you're my girl," Ginger said, and they laughed.

Serena's words helped Ginger at least let down her guard enough to observe Paul and his actions with an objective eye, not a tainted one. And that allowed her to agree to the trip and to go with an open mind to enjoy it.

She did quietly wonder how three-and-a-half days with her mother and her mother-in-law would pass without someone looking to pull out someone's hair. But she was up to the challenge because the trip very well could be the turning point in her marriage, which she wanted to get back on track.

Paul wanted that, too, and he was in a good place in his life, finally. He was with his beloved wife on their dream trip, even as she remained suspect about him. He had lost ten pounds since receiving the lottery check and discarded the cloud that hung over him. He was rich. And, above all, he had hope.

He did have a bit of drama, though: the way he saw it, his wife had not totally fallen back in line; indeed, she carried a bit of an attitude with her to California. But he could work on that. His mom and Ginger's mom represented a different story. They had not seen each other in months and that time apart did not temper their issues.

From the start, they did not agree that their children should marry. Brenda Wall saw Ginger as an overly emotional weakling who only sought a husband, not a true mate.

"I don't trust her," she told Paul at the time. "There's something about her that is sneaky and underhanded. And you told me she can't have children, right? So, why would you want to marry someone who cannot bear your children?"

"Because I love her, Ma," Paul said. "Because I am better with her than without her. Because we match and enjoy each other and have the same ideas about life. I'm almost ashamed that you're telling me to not marry someone I love because she can't have children, like that's all there is to life and happiness."

Brenda accepted her son's position, but she never agreed with it. And so, she treated Ginger with disdain or disregard, albeit not overtly. When they adopted Helena, the new grandmother said at a gathering of family and friends: "I'm so proud of you, Paul. You're going to be a great parent and instill all the character in this child that she needs."

She did not mention Ginger, and Ginger's mom was incensed. She told her daughter in the kitchen, when they were alone and away from the guests: "This woman is sick. How dare her ignore your role in your baby's life. I don't have a problem with Paul. But that mother of his…going around talking about God this and God that. In reality, she's Lucifer. Let her disrespect you like that again and I'm—"

"You're gonna what, Ma? Fight her?" Ginger asked. "That's not happening. You're too old to be even talking about something like that. She might have a problem with me, but we're gonna take the high road. Momma, I'm a mother. I have a baby. We shouldn't even be talking about that woman right now."

And the talk ended there, but the animosity did not. They were around each other for special occasions like Helena's graduation from high school, and they had token conversation. This would have to change over the trip, and neither Paul nor Ginger knew in what way.

A sense of what was to come occurred at the Atlanta airport. Ginger's mother, Madeline, was a bit taken aback by the Southwest Airlines boarding procedure—first-come-first served—and complained about it to her daughter for twenty minutes. Finally, Ginger told her: "Mother, we're gonna get on the plane and that's it. It's Thanksgiving morning. Let's be thankful for this.

"Plus," she added, "you're a senior. You can board before everyone else."

That logic brought down Madeline's emotions. "It could be worse," she said. "I could be sitting next to Brenda."

"Momma," Ginger said, "you're sharing a room with her in Napa. So, what's wrong with sitting next to her on the flight? We're not gonna have any nonsense on this trip. Right? *Right?*"

Madeline reluctantly nodded her heard.

"This is an important trip," Ginger said. "We're going to a beautiful place. We're a family. Let's enjoy it and not mess it up with petty stuff. I don't get along that great with Mrs. Wall, either. But I don't let it bother me. I do what I believe is the right thing and keep it moving. You should adopt the same attitude."

"Yeah, well, we'll see," Madeline said. "She thinks her son is all that, that he's too good for you. And here he is, he can't even keep a job."

"Mother," Ginger jumped in. She found herself defending her husband, which was not the plan. Her position was more about altering her mother's attitude than taking up for Paul.

"Paul has worked all his life," she said. "He got laid off. It's been a tough economy lately. But he still worked hard to provide for us. You need to stop looking at him as a failure. He could have given up or sat back and collected unemployment. But he didn't. It hasn't been easy for him. But he's hung there."

She said all that and yet she at times felt about Paul exactly as her mom did. But the wife in her would not allow anyone, not even her mother, to bad-mouth her husband.

"If you say so," Madeline allowed.

"Momma, you can get on the plane now," Ginger said. "I'm in Group B, so I will be on later. Why don't you sit with Mrs. Hall?"

"What?" Madeline said. "No way. She left to go to the little store over there and didn't even ask if I wanted anything. She only cares about herself."

"Momma, you were in the bathroom when she went to the store; so how could she ask you if you wanted something?" Ginger said. "And why can't you walk over there and get something if you want something? See, this is what I'm talking about, Momma. This is unnecessary drama you're trying to create and that's not good."

"Well, I'm still not sitting next to her," she said. "I will hold a seat for you."

"Momma, what about Paul?"

"What about him? He can sit with his mother," Madeline said.

In the store, as they sought reading material for the flight, Brenda Wall said, "This is a long flight; I hope you plan to sit with me."

"Why you say that, Ma?" Paul asked.

"Because I don't want to sit next to a stranger; you

never know who those people are," she said. "I don't want to have to fake small talk with someone I'll never see again."

"Then read and go to sleep," Paul said. "No one said you have to talk to anyone. And why don't you sit with Ms. Price anyway?"

"No way," she snapped. "I'd rather sit on the wing."

"Ma, I have enough anxiety already; I hate to fly," he said. "I haven't been on a plane in ten years and I'm not that excited about getting back on one now. And you're complaining about sitting beside strangers? Sit with Ms. Price and you'll see she's not nearly as bad as you think."

"She's a borderline alcoholic who would go anywhere alcohol is being served," Brenda said. "And you want me to sit with her as she drinks for five hours?"

"Yes," Paul said, "I do. I want you to and I need you to at least try to get along with her. I bet you'll find that you all hate the same things."

"Is that supposed to be funny?" she said, while purchasing a fashion magazine. "What are you saying? That I'm negative? That I'm like her?"

"All I'm saying is that you probably have similar interests and could probably at least learn a little more about each other. Maybe that will help you all act more like family toward each other."

As it would turn out, with Southwest's open seating policy, the in-laws were unable to sit together, even if they wanted. But that did not mean it was a smooth flight for any of them.

CHAPTER 5
UP, UP
AND AWAY

Minutes before the doors were shut on the plane, Paul went to the men's room and splashed his face with water. He took some Dramamine and talked to himself about enjoying the experience of flying as opposed to fearing it. He read something on the Internet about that approach.

And it worked. He stepped onto the plane feeling at ease and confident. Paul chewed the gum in his mouth at a furious pace, but it helped calm him. There were no seats near the front, so he managed his way near the back, where he found a center seat between a young man who seemed to be hung over and an older woman who was working on a crossword puzzle.

He thought, *This guy is sleeping and this lady is doing a word game—it's going to be fine.*

And it was—for a while. Paul's heart pounded as the jet picked up speed on the runway. He held on to the armrests with a death grip. His body constricted and his breathing was impaired. He began to sweat. And he even started to feel nauseous.

The guy and senior on either side of him did not notice his issues. And when the plane elevated from the ground, Paul began to feel more and more at ease. He looked around and only he seemed uptight about the take off. Many passengers were already asleep; others seemed totally unconcerned.

Finally, Paul calmed all the way down to where he eventually dozed off. He felt accomplished. He had conquered his fear. He was flying to California. When he woke up, he looked around and found Ginger across the aisle two rows in front of him. He didn't even notice her as he entered the plane; he was so wound up with anxiety.

He waved at her and she nodded her head in a reassuring way. She wanted to take Serena's advice and embrace reconciliation. But it was not easy. Being stubborn and prideful remained a part of her disposition. But she fought her instincts.

Ginger got up from her seat and came over to Paul's row. "How you feeling?" she asked. She said it in a loving way, a way Paul had not heard from her in some time. It made him feel like his wife was coming back to him. She cared.

"I'm not on the floor curled up in the fetal position, so I guess I'm OK," he said.

Ginger laughed, and Paul's world lit up. When he was in his rational mind, he loved to make her laugh; it made both of them feel good. He had forgotten how much he enjoyed that because he had not heard her laugh in months.

"Good," she said. "Get some rest. That'll make the trip shorter."

She went back to her seat and checked on her mom, who was sitting directly in front of her, on the aisle. Ginger leaned forward and her mom leaned back so her ear could meet her daughter's mouth.

"Is that alcohol I smell on your breath?" Ginger whispered. "How can that be? They haven't even started the beverage service yet?"

"Why I have to wait on them?" Madeline Price said, showing Ginger a small plastic bottle in her purse. "It's legal. It's the right size to take as a carryon. And who are you anyway? I'm the mother."

"Well, it would be nice if you acted like it," Ginger said.

"What did I do now?" Madeline asked.

"Why can't you wait until they bring you drinks?" Ginger said. "Do you have to bring drinks with you? It's not even eleven o'clock and you're drinking. We're going to Napa Valley, for Christ's sakes."

"Don't you get snappy with me, girl," her mother responded, almost turning completely around in her chair. "You watch your mouth with me. If I want to drink now, I will drink now. I don't need your permission or anyone else's."

She then reached into her purse, pulled out her little stash and took a swig. Ginger dropped back in her seat, frustrated and angry and was not sure which emotion was more prominent.

Maybe we should have left her at home, she thought to herself.

At the same time, Brenda Wall was seething. She had

a window seat, but the man next to her smelled of some kind of vinegar, from his mouth and pores. And he would not stop talking.

"I live in the South because the people are nicer," he said to Brenda. "You said you're going to Napa. You're gonna love it. I would start off slow. That's where first-timers make the mistake. They come in so excited that they shoot their whole wad at the first winery. Big mistake.

"You have to pace yourself. Enjoy wherever you go first, but realize that's only the first one. You don't have to try to get drunk on your first visit. There is nothing out there if there isn't wine. So, it's not like they're going to run out of it, you know?

"I like the smaller vineyards over the big ones. Small ones like—you want me to write this down for you?— Black Coyote and Brown are very underrated. But the big ones aren't overrated. Mondavi, Beringer, Mumm's… they are all good. Really, you can't go wrong out there. I realize you've probably done your research. You look like a woman who plans things out thoroughly, to every detail.

"Am I right?"

Before Brenda could answer, he jumped in and went on.

"Of course, I'm right. But, still, when you're going somewhere you don't know, local knowledge is very important. So be sure to contact the concierge of your hotel and anyone you run into who lives out there. They'll really give you someplace that will be nice…"

He went on for another five minutes before taking a breath. She had long since stopped hearing what he was saying and was seething that he would besiege her with chatter—and an aroma that insulted her senses. When he took that pause, she finally jumped in.

"Thanks for all that info," she said as politely as she could. "I will put it to good use. Now I'm going to get some sleep so I can have some energy when we get there."

She was relieved to get that out, but it did not stop her neighbor.

"Sleeping on planes is overrated," he said. "You're not comfortable, you're probably going to get a stiff neck and that doesn't feel good. Plus, sleep on a plane is fake sleep; it only fools you to believe you are rested when you really are not. So, pretty soon after you get off the plane, you'll crash.

"I make sure I get my rest before my flight, no matter how early it is. That way, I don't have to worry about sleeping or being rested when I get to the other end. You get what I'm saying?

"Now, some people—and you might be one of them— can sleep on a plane as they do in their beds. Not me. My arm goes to sleep. My knees get achy. My head is jerking all over the place. Me, I like to sit here and meet nice people and talk and learn something and take in the view and enjoy a great experience that way…"

Brenda was beside herself. She told the man she wanted to go to sleep and he ignored her and continued to talk—

and shoot that disgusting smell in her direction. She did not know what to do. At an earlier time in her life, she would have stopped the man in mid-sentence and let him know he was annoying her. But as she got older and seriously involved in the church, she softened a little.

So, instead of humiliating the man, she pretended to fall asleep as he rambled. She slowly closed her eyes and even let her head drift forward. She had to hold back laughing at herself. Still, while it was funny to her, to the guy it was another reason for him to talk.

"Hey, watch it," he said. "You're falling asleep. That's what I'm talking about. Your head jerked, you were kind of suspended. Any minute you were going to be slobbering all over yourself. And that wouldn't have been pretty. See what I'm saying?

"One time I saw this man snore on a plane. He had stuff dripping out of his mouth. He was a mess. And when he woke up, guess what he said: That he was tired. All that snoring and everything and he still felt sluggish. Best thing to do is to get some rest and a light meal for the flight and you'll be fine. You won't need to try to go to sleep in this tight little space.

"The best thing—"

Brenda couldn't take it anymore. She stopped him in the middle of another monologue. "Excuse me," she said. "I have to go to the bathroom."

Even with that, the man continued to talk. "Good luck in that little space in there," he started. "I have heard of a case where a particularly large person got stuck in there.

It took two flight attendants and a passenger to pull him out."

"Excuse me," Brenda said again, sounding exasperated as she unbuckled her seat belt. "I've really got to go."

Finally, she was free, and when she reached the aisle, she let out a sigh of relief. Oddly enough, there was but one free seat on the plane—next to her son's mother-in-law, Madeline. It was a center seat that became vacant just as she got up from her seat, as that woman moved to the only other open seat on the plane, a few rows up near a friend.

So Brenda had a choice: to return to sit next to stinky mouth-all-mighty or to sit next to Madeline, who she did not like. It was a tough choice. Before she decided, though, she asked Ginger if she wanted to take the seat next to her mother, which would give Brenda Ginger's seat.

"No, thank you," Ginger said without hesitation. "It's all yours."

Damn, Brenda thought. *Her own daughter doesn't want to sit next to her. Why should I?*

She went a couple rows back to check on Paul, who was sleeping. That relieved her because she was concerned about his paranoia around flying. After the bathroom visit, she decided she could not bear another few hours next to the loquacious man. So she swallowed hard and asked Madeline to allow her past so she could take the now-empty center seat next to her.

Madeline was shocked, but obliged. As she stood up to let Brenda into the aisle, Paul woke up. The women were face to face in the cramped aisle, and to Paul it looked like a confrontation. And he panicked.

"No," he yelled, and everyone turned to him. "Stop. Stop."

"Paul," Brenda said.

"No, I don't want to hear it," Paul answered. He unbuckled his seat belt and climbed over the sleepy-headed guy next to him and stumbled into the aisle, bumping into a seated passenger.

He hurried over to his mother and mother-in-law and separated them. "Why can't you just simply get along?" he said. "This is silly. You're fighting on a plane?"

"Paul," Ginger said, pulling him by the arm. "No one is fighting."

"I saw it; they were in each other's face," he said. "And I heard them yelling."

"Honey," his wife said, "you were dreaming. They weren't fighting."

"Is there a problem?" a flight attendant asked.

Paul looked around confused. "Maybe I was dreaming," he said. "I'm sorry. I think I dreamed that you all were fighting and then I woke up and there you were, in each other's face... I'm sorry."

Before he could ask for a cup of water, the plane hit some turbulence and rocked. Right away, Paul was panicked again, only worse—and Ginger knew it. She could see it in his eyes, which darted back and forth.

"Come on, sit back down," she said, guiding Paul back to his seat.

"What's going on?" he said. "What was that?"

"A little turbulence, that's all," the flight attendant said.

"But why? Why is the plane shaking?" he asked.

The flight attendant got him secure in his seat before answering. "It's just that we're going through some clouds or some wind bursts," she said. "Nothing big."

"Dude, you gonna be OK? You ain't gon' throw up on me, are you?" the sleepy guy next to him said. Paul did not answer.

The captain came over the intercom. "Folks, please strap yourselves in. We have some rough spots up ahead that will make it a little bumpy. But we'll be fine. It should only last about five minutes."

Those five minutes seemed much longer to Paul. All the good feelings he mustered up diminished. He reached up to open the air vent above his seat; he was getting hot, sweating profusely and he felt as if the cabin was shrinking around him.

In his panic, he wondered how the lady to his right could continue to fiddle with the puzzle and how the guy next to him fell right back to sleep. The plane not only was jumping, but it was spinning, too, at least in his mind. He felt like he was drunk off of two bottles of Shiraz, but was also fiercely scared.

Paul decided he would close his eyes and hold on. He started reciting a poem he memorized called "Invictus," by William Ernest Henley:

Out of the night that covers me,
Black as the Pit from pole to pole,

I thank whatever gods may be
For my unconquerable soul.
In the fell clutch of circumstance
I have not winced nor cried aloud.
Under the bludgeonings of chance
My head is bloody, but unbowed.
Beyond this place of wrath and tears
Looms but the Horror of the shade,
And yet the menace of the years
Finds, and shall find, me unafraid.
It matters not how strait the gate,
How charged with punishments the scroll.
I am the master of my fate:
I am the captain of my soul.

In focusing on the words, Paul's attention was off the turbulence. And while he was far from comfortable, he did stop sweating.

He recited the poem over and over until, finally, the plane stabilized; they were out of the turbulent area. Paul did not open his eyes, though. He kept them closed, hoping that he would drift off to sleep so he wouldn't have to deal with anything else that could come.

And there was more to come. His mother and mother in-law, sitting side-by-side, got along like a mongoose and a snake.

"What's wrong with him?" Madeline asked Brenda, which was not a good thing to ask.

"What's wrong with *you*?" Brenda replied. "You smell like a bottle of Scotch."

"Actually, it's cognac," Madeline said. "You know the last time I was on vacation? Do you know what's been going on in my life? And do you know that I am sixty-four years old? I can drink whatever I want, whenever I want."

"Who said you couldn't?" Brenda asked. "I wanted to know if you have a drinking problem. We're going to the wine country. I mean, we will be drinking a lot."

"I have always been respectful of you, and I don't want to not be respectful now," Madeline said. "But I really don't give a damn what you think. I lost my husband of forty-four years less than a year ago. Do you have any idea what that is like?"

"Actually, I do, sort of," Brenda said. "I lost my second husband—my first marriage lasted a year; we were both too young. I woke up one morning and said I didn't want to be married anymore. And just like that, it was over. So, yeah, I understand exactly what you mean. My husband didn't die, but he might as well had. Shit, I wish he were dead because I feel like I wasted a lot of years with him."

Madeline laughed. It was one of the few times they shared a laugh in the twenty years they knew each other. She then twisted the lid off her stash of Remy Martin and handed it to Brenda.

"Go ahead," Madeline said. "You could use it."

Brenda stared at it for a few seconds, reached over and took a swig. She curled up her face. "This is too strong for me," she said. "But it did warm me up."

They laughed again. And whatever animosity they held for each other subsided with each turn they took downing the alcohol.

Ginger sat a row behind them, watching in disbelief. She did not know what to think, how to feel. She thought: *Wow, it is great to see them actually talking and laughing. But is my mother corrupting Ms. Wall? This is crazy.*

She shook her head. She was in a crossfire of drama. To her right and two rows behind her was her husband with his eyes closed reciting a poem. In front of her were her mom and mother-in-law getting drunk.

This is gonna be some trip, she said to herself.

CHAPTER 6
TOUCH
DOWN

It was a rough landing. The wind off the San Francisco Bay rocked the plane on its approach to the landing strip. Paul closed his eyes tighter and recited the poem louder.

And when the pilot got it on the ground, it was as if it were dropped from the sky.

Boom!

So hard was the landing that an overhead bin opened up on impact. None of this made Paul feel good about the prospect of having to fly back home in a few days.

People clapped that the plane was safely on the runway, and Paul was confused. "They're clapping for *that* landing. I damn near got whiplash," he said aloud.

"No, dude," the guy that had slept nearly the entire flight said. "We're clapping for being safe. You never flew before?"

"Long time ago, when I was a kid and didn't know any better," he said.

"Don't sweat it, man," the guy said. "Go to sleep. It shortens the trip."

"Up in the air is not the place to be," Paul said. "But I hear you."

His and Ginger's eyes met, and she offered him a reassuring smile that said, "You did it."

He smiled back—and then looked right ahead of Ginger and noticed his mom and Madeline chatting as if they were old, close friends.

"Well, I'll be damned," he said. "Gin?…"

His wife looked at him, shook her head and hunched her shoulders. Then she did the motion with her hand toward her mouth to indicate they had been drinking. Paul rolled his eyes and grew concerned. The impact of alcohol could take it one of two ways, and one of them was not good.

But to see them getting along made Ginger and Paul feel good—even if it was alcohol-induced.

"I see we're gonna have to keep them drunk to make sure this is a good trip," Ginger said to Paul when they exited the plane.

"Maybe I should get drunk before the flight back," he said.

"You did good," Ginger responded. "It was a little rough for you in the beginning, but it got better. I'm proud of you. How do you feel?"

"Not as good as them," he said, looking at Brenda and Madeline. "You're right; gotta keep them drunk."

"That shouldn't be hard considering where we're going," Ginger said.

They walked over to their parents, who were giggling like schoolgirls.

"How's it going?" Paul asked.

"Great," the parents said in unison.

Paul and Ginger looked at each other and smiled.

"Let's pick up the bags and then go rent the car," Paul said.

"I need to go to the bathroom," Madeline said.

"I'll go with you," Brenda said, and off they went.

"Am I in the Twilight Zone or something?" Ginger said.

"Hey, let's ride it out. It might not last," Paul said.

Paul was right. By the time they picked up the luggage and started up the 101 Freeway toward San Francisco, it started to change.

"It's about ninety minutes to get to Napa," Brenda said. "We should stop in San Francisco and find someplace to watch the game."

"The game?" Madeline asked. "What game?"

"The Redskins are playing the Cowboys," Brenda answered. "We are Redskins fans in my house."

"That's not a bad idea, Ma," Paul said. "And we can get something to eat, too."

"Aren't we having Thanksgiving dinner at the hotel?" Madeline said.

"Yes, but it's only two o'clock now," Brenda said. "Dinner is at eight-thirty."

"At eight-thirty?" Madeline said. "That's eleven-thirty East Coast time. That's too late."

"So you want to have Thanksgiving dinner now?" Brenda asked.

And back and forth they went for another two minutes, the dialogue increasing in contention as they went on. Paul glanced over at Ginger, who closed her eyes and shook her head.

"Mother," Ginger chimed in, "what's wrong with stopping in San Francisco and having lunch? You have never been to San Francisco. I haven't either. It'll be a shame to drive past it without at least stopping for a short time."

"Look," Madeline said, pointing to the dramatic skyline of San Francisco off in the distance. "There. You've seen it. Let's get to where we came out here to visit."

"Don't worry," Brenda said, "I'm sure there is alcohol in San Francisco, too."

And it went from contentious to ugly in warp speed.

All the chumminess developed on the end of the flight was crushed. Madeline was irate. It didn't help that she still had a slight buzz from the drinking. It heightened her emotions.

"You have some nerve, Brenda," Madeline said. "You sat there and drank most of my stash and had two— wait—three other drinks. That's just like an alcoholic to try to point attention at someone else."

"Alcoholic? I was only drinking so you wouldn't drink that whole thing by yourself and get crazy behind it," Brenda said. "And I didn't drink most of that cheap liquor you had. Tasted like spoiled Witch Hazel."

Madeline was ready to go "ham," as the kids say, when Ginger jumped in. "OK, OK," she said. "Not in front of the children."

Paul burst into laughter, hoping his action would charge the parents to calm down, at least a little. It worked. Well, sort of. They stopped bickering but stopped talking altogether.

They moved away from each other, up against the back doors of the rented Monte Carlo.

"Mrs. Price, I hope you don't mind if we do stop in the city," Paul said. "I'd like to see the game and I'm hungry. Aren't you? It's Thanksgiving afternoon, but we should be able to find someplace where we can eat and watch the game."

"I think we're all probably a little irritable because we're hungry," Ginger chimed in. "And I don't particularly care to watch the game. But I'd like to see San Francisco. Let's go down to Union Square. I read about it. We should be able to find a place to eat with some TVs, too."

The parents in the backseat did not say a word. They looked out of their respective windows, seething.

Paul and Ginger were disappointed that the harmony did not last an hour. Ginger turned on the radio and searched for songs that would promote a good mood.

They hit near-standstill traffic about five miles from downtown—surprising for Thanksgiving afternoon. "Can you believe this?" Paul asked, looking over his shoulder at the in-laws. Neither responded.

It was then that Ginger, ironically enough, found a song on the radio that fit the occasion: "We Are Family" by Sister Sledge.

She turned up the volume on the song and started to sing along with it. So did Paul.

The parents looked at their kids with disdain.

When the song ended, Paul decided to give the seniors a speech for them to consider.

"That song came on at the right time," he said. "We are supposed to be reminded that we are a family. Like it or not, that's what we are. And we're doing something most families don't get a chance to do.

"We're taking a trip together as a family. In the end, that's all we have. We are the people we should be able to rely on. And we shouldn't be at each other's throats. Especially today. How can we, on Thanksgiving, sit up here and listen to our parents go at it like enemies? That's not right."

"I cannot believe it, to be honest," Ginger contributed. "Although we are adults, parents never stop teaching and being parents. This is a bad example. Helena will get married one day and I hope to God Paul and I do not behave with her in-laws as you are. It doesn't make any sense. We respect you so much. But this is disappointing."

The women felt foolish, but did not respond.

Paul waited a few minutes before saying anything else. They had arrived in downtown San Francisco. They maneuvered up and down the hilly streets toward Union Square. Instead of piling it on, he decided his place was to leave it alone and show his mother respect. Under any circumstance, he would honor his mom.

"Welcome to San Francisco," he said. "I can't believe I am here. I heard so much about it, seen it on TV. To be here…"

"It's very nice," Ginger added.

Paul decided to park in a lot right in Union Square, across from Macy's. A prodigious Christmas tree with big, colorful bulbs rested in the center of the square, adjacent to an ice-skating rink.

The mild weather—temperatures in the mid-sixties—promoted walking, and there were many people out on Thanksgiving after-noon milling about.

Paul walked from the underground lot with his arm around his mother's shoulder and Ginger locked arms with Madeline.

"Ma, we're in San Francisco," Paul said. "How awesome is this?"

"It is beautiful," she said. "I didn't tell you earlier, but I will say it now, son. I'm proud of you to get on that plane. I read all about people who have a fear of flying. Do you know most of them never conquer it? But you have. I'm proud of you."

"Thanks, Ma," Paul said. "It wasn't easy. I hated it, to be honest. But I did it."

Behind them, Madeline said to her daughter: "See what I mean? She thinks she's better than us, trying to talk about my drinking when she probably had more than me."

"Mother, it doesn't even matter," Ginger said. "Like you told me, you are grown and can drink what you want.

We don't need her approval. I simply don't want you to let something she—or anyone, for that matter—says influence your trip. This is supposed to be a great trip."

"You're right, honey, and that's what it will be," Madeline said. "People make me shake my head."

They walked around the square and up the hill, past an Italian restaurant, Scoma's, which was closed. The doorman at the small hotel suggested a diner on the corner, a small spot across the street or an Italian restaurant around the corner. But Ginger spotted a Marriott.

"They should have a bar and restaurant, right?" she said.

"Let's try it out," her mother said.

Not only that, but they had the Redskins game on, too.

"Ma, this is perfect, right?" Paul said.

That comment annoyed Ginger. It was as if he was still seeking his mother's approval.

"Perfect," his mom said. "Things have a way of working out."

They took a table near the bar and the server distributed menus.

"Can I take the liberty and ordering something to drink for everyone?" Paul asked.

No one contested, so he ordered a bottle of St. Supery Chardonnay, 2009. "It's buttery and has a citrus taste, but not sweet," Paul explained. "They have a winery in Napa. We have to check it out."

"Sounds like it will go well with a burger," his mom said.

"See, you're trying to be funny, but it actually does go well with beef," Paul said. "Usually I'd go with a red wine with beef. But this chardonnay will work because for me, it's really—it's about what tastes good."

"What do you think, Mother?" Ginger asked. "When is the last time you had a burger?"

"Probably when you were a baby," she answered. "Maybe a burger would be good."

"How about it?" Paul asked his mother.

"Fine," Brenda said.

And so, they all ordered burgers. The wine came and Paul poured and then made a toast as everyone lifted a glass.

"Happy Thanksgiving," he started. "To love and family and happiness."

"That's it?" Ginger asked.

"Isn't that enough?" he answered.

"You know what? You're right," she said, and they all tapped glasses, even Madeline and Brenda.

Paul and Brenda were into the football game on the TV in front of their table like two buddies would be. The mother was as passionate about the Redskins as the son, making commentary with every play and hanging on to every action on the field.

When a commercial came, Paul noticed that it was still awkward with the in-laws not speaking to each other. At the same time, the more they sipped, the more the wine began to take a toll.

"Y'all need to keep some of that noise down," Madeline finally said to Paul and Brenda.

"Are we loud?" Paul asked. He had not eaten in ten hours, so the wine went straight to his head. All of them, in fact, were buzzing.

"Yeah, you are, a little," Ginger said.

"Well, when you watch a football game, you can't sit here all quiet," Brenda said. "And there's hardly anyone in here. We're not bothering anybody."

"Well, you're bothering me," Madeline said.

"Oh, I'm sorry," Brenda said. "I didn't realize your ears were so sensitive."

"Well, they are," Madeline said.

"Perhaps you should go on the other side—there's no one over there," Brenda said. "It's perfectly quiet. You won't be missed."

"Wait," Ginger said before her mom responded. "On the plane, you all were laughing and talking and getting along. What were you talking about? What was so funny?"

Her questions stumped them. They wanted to remember, but couldn't. The wine had them going. They looked at each other and laughed.

"You don't remember?" Brenda asked.

"Well, I think... Weren't we talking about... Didn't you say..." Madeline said, unable to complete a thought.

"Oh, I remember one thing," Brenda said. "You said your husband died and I said I wished mine had died."

"Oh, yeah," Madeline said, laughing.

"Paul, pour us some more wine," Brenda told her son.

"Ma, you said you wish Dad was dead?" Paul asked. He was serious. He maintained a close relationship with his father, who retired to Palm Beach, Florida. He had planned to remarry in the next year.

"He is dead to me," Brenda said. She reached for the bottle, but it was empty. The server was standing there to alert them the food would arrive shortly.

"Bring us another bottle of this," Brenda to the server.

"He's dead to you is different from wishing he were dead," Paul said.

"I don't wish no harm on the man," she said. "Not anymore."

Which led Paul to ask the question he not dare ask sober.

"So, Ma, why did you really get a divorce?" he said. "I mean, thirty-something, forty years, whatever it was. What could be that bad? Did he cheat on you? I asked him that and he said he didn't? Did you cheat on him? He said you didn't. So what was it?"

Brenda Wall wanted to tell her son the truth but had not. The wine made it easier for the truth to flow out of her mouth.

"I didn't love him," she said. "I had stopped loving your dad probably ten, twelve years ago."

"What?" Ginger said. She was feeling bold, too, and jumped into the conversation. "How can that be? How can you stay married to someone that long and not love him? I don't understand."

"Some things aren't meant for you to understand,"

Brenda said. "I hope you don't ever understand. If you do, then that would mean you don't love my son, because the only way to really understand is to be in a situation like I was. That's the only way."

"Ma, I was around you guys all my life," Paul said. "I didn't see anything that made me feel like you all didn't love each other."

"We did love each other," Brenda explained. "But we were not *in* love. That ended a long time ago. It faded away, like smoke, into the air. Gone. And I believe it hit both of us around the same time. There was no spark, no magic."

The second bottle of wine came and Paul refilled the glasses. Brenda went on.

"We stayed together for one reason: loyalty. We were best friends at one time and we saw each other through some serious issues that brought us closer together."

"Like what, Ma?" Paul said. "This is blowing my mind and I'm trying to understand."

Brenda Wall sipped her wine and closed her eyes. The room was rotating and she was trying to stop it—and her tongue. It didn't work.

She sat back in her chair and took a deep breath. "When you were a baby, too young to even understand what was happening," Brenda explained, "I was very sick. Doctors didn't know what was wrong with me, but I couldn't keep any food down and I lost weight like crazy and was tired all the time.

"Finally, I went to the hospital; stayed there for eleven days. They ran all kinds of tests, but couldn't find anything. They thought it might be lupus at one point. They tried all the experimental drugs on me.

"Your father was right there with me, in the hospital, taking care of you. He was totally positive; he kept my head up. If he hadn't, I think I would have died. Seriously. Altogether, I was sick for about three weeks. I mean, really sick. When they sent me home, your father carried me from the bed to the bathroom. He cleaned up after me. He did everything. And he never complained.

"The doctors finally put me on some kind of steroids, and I finally started feeling better. Do you know what it's like to feel like you're going to die? To feel like you're fading away? Here I was with a precious little boy and I was dying. That's what I believed. And I cried my eyes out every night. And your father held me in his arms every night—until, finally, the steroids, did something to right the ship."

"He did that out of love, Ms. Wall," Ginger said. "That's beautiful."

"It was beautiful," Brenda said. "But over time, it all faded. Why? How? Because, really, being totally honest, he wasn't the man for me."

"What do you mean, Ma?"

"I mean…" Brenda said, taking a deep breath, "when I was pregnant with you, I wasn't sure your father was your father."

"What? What do you mean?" Paul said.

"I mean that I was dating someone else, in love with someone else, when I got pregnant by your dad," Brenda said. Suddenly, she became almost sullen. She sipped more wine and spewed more truths, truths she never thought she would share with her son.

"The man I was in love with was special to me," she explained. "We were young and in love and used to talk all the time about the life we would have. But he got drafted into the Army and before I knew it, he was gone.

"He wrote me and I wrote him, but he wasn't sure when he was going to come back home. Finally, he did come back home, and nothing changed. He was fun and exciting and he loved me. We had fun for about a week before he had to go back.

"He was stationed in North Carolina but was going overseas somewhere, Germany, I think. We were barely twenty years old. I was mad that he left and, at a most vulnerable point, I met your father. He was the friend of a coworker. He was outside our building when we got off work, waiting for his friend, who I was walking with.

"He invited me to go out with them, and I did. And it grew from there.

"A little while later—about a month or two—I realized I didn't have my regular cycle. And that's where the confusion came in. But when the doctors told me how long I had been pregnant, I knew it was James' baby."

"Why is it I never heard this before?" Paul asked.

"I don't know," his mother said. "It's not a good story, really. When he came back home, I was eight months pregnant and it broke his heart when I told him he wasn't the father. And it broke my heart, too. I should have waited on him, but I really didn't think I would see him again. My friends were telling me, 'Brenda, he's going to travel the world and you think he's coming back to you?' And after hearing it enough, I started to believe it."

"Where is he now?" Madeline asked.

"I don't know," Brenda said. "After I told him I was pregnant, he still wanted to marry me. That's the kind of man he was. But I had already made plans to marry James and I thought it wouldn't be fair to you, Paul, to not have your father in your life. My friend understood, but he had tears in his eyes when he left me. And I cried."

Brenda actually developed tears in her eyes as she told the story. And Paul noticed.

"You still love him, don't you, Ma?" he asked.

She wiped her face. "I guess I still love the idea of him and what we could have had together," Brenda said. "But your father and I got married before you were born— yes, I went down that aisle with a big ole stomach—and went on and had a good life together for a long time."

"But it wasn't what you planned for yourself?" Paul asked.

"It wasn't; but you have to walk in your life. It is already planned for us," his mom said. "James was a good man; *is* a good man. I was joking about wanting him dead.

That would devastate me. But he wasn't *the* man for me. And over time, it just got to be that I had to breathe again. I couldn't breathe being in a marriage that really didn't do anything for me.

"We had our greatest gift—you—and some really good times, times I will never forget. But you were long gone and I was left dealing with the man in front of me. And that wasn't enough—for either of us."

"Don't you feel lonely, though?" Madeline asked. "I know I do."

"Yes, you're right," Brenda admitted. "At times it's very lonely. But the peace I have within myself balances it out."

The burgers came and they ate mostly in silence—except for an occasional outburst by Paul about the football game. They enjoyed the meal and the wine and watched the Redskins defeat the Cowboys, giving mother and son some needed feel-good after Brenda's revelations.

On the way back to the car, Paul walked with Ginger and Brenda with Madeline, and the drama seemed to fade away…for a while, anyway.

CHAPTER 7
IN THE LAND
OF GRAPES

P aul settled into the car and headed toward
Napa. His GPS gave him directions across the
Bay Bridge, but he wanted to cross the Golden
Gate Bridge.

And, surprisingly, no one argued with him.

After some wayward turns in the city, though, Ginger
asked: "Can I ask someone how we get to the Golden
Gate? We're wasting time."

"My instincts tell me we're close," Paul said.

"Boy, you have the sense of direction of a blind donkey,"
his mother said. "Ask somebody so we can stop riding
around this city."

"Really," Madeline said. "I'm ready for a hot shower
and…"

"And what?" Brenda asked with a smile. "Go ahead,
you can say it."

"A drink, dammit. Get a drink," Madeline blurted out,
and everyone laughed. Well, everyone except Ginger. She
had some concern about her mother's drinking, and it
increased by the month. Based on what she saw on the
plane and at lunch, Ginger was now worried.

Her mother always had a healthy appetite for cocktails, but it grew exponentially after her husband died less than a year before.

"Mother, maybe we should start fresh tomorrow when we visit the vineyards," she said. It was as delicately as she could put it.

"Excuse me?" Madeline said.

"I'm just saying that we have a lot of sipping to do and I don't want you to be sick tomorrow because you had so much today," Ginger said.

Madeline was already buzzing from the wine at lunch, and it showed. "I thought we already talked about this," she said to her daughter. "I don't need nobody monitoring how much I drink. You act like I'm gonna get sloppy drunk and embarrass you. Well, I won't.

"And if I did embarrass you it would be payback for all the times you embarrassed the hell out of me when you were a kid."

Paul found the Golden Gate Bridge, without anyone's assistance, and made sure everyone knew it. "Who told you it was close?" he said, "Me. I have the instincts of an explorer."

He said that to turn the subject; he could sense it was getting heated between mother and daughter. Didn't work.

"So that's your excuse, Mother?" Ginger said. The way she said it made Paul look at his wife. It was dark in the car, so he fumbled with the gadgets around the rearview mirror until he found the interior light switch.

He wanted to see Ginger's eyes; they told if she were intoxicated. If they were open and bright, she was OK. If they were barely open and glazed over…trouble. Some people get quiet when they get a buzz, some get loud, some get talkative, some get belligerent. Ginger was one of the belligerent ones.

"You're paying me back for what I did as a child?" she asked. "Really? Seriously? You're joking, right? I can recall some things that you did to me when I was a child that I should be mad at you about, if you want to know the truth."

"The truth is that—look—we're about to cross the Golden Gate Bridge," Paul said, again trying to get their attention somewhere else. The women turned to look, but only briefly.

"Look," Brenda said, "you can walk across the bridge. We should do that—well not you, Paul. But I think I would do it."

"Yeah, I can do without that, Ma," he said. "Oh, wow. Look over there."

He pointed to his far right, where across the San Francisco Bay you could see the beautiful skyline of San Francisco all lit up.

"Now that's beautiful," Brenda said. "Do you ladies see this?"

Ginger and Madeline turned and admired the spectacular view. Paul drove slowly so they could take in as much of it as possible.

"The East Coast is not this pretty," Madeline said. "The mountains, the water, the skyline—this is so gorgeous."

The banter about the beauty of the area continued across the bridge and along Interstate 80. Ginger was about to address her mother again when Paul said to her: "You're up front, so you have to be my navigator. How long are we on this highway?"

It was a nice try, but Ginger was looking for a confrontation. "Here," she said to Paul, handing him her cell phone. "I programmed the hotel's address in the GPS. That will get us there."

She then turned halfway around in her seat to address her mother.

"I wasn't the one as a five-year-old kid who was left at home alone," she said. "I can recall many times when I wasn't even in the first grade and Daddy was at work and you locked me in the house and went to do God knows what."

"Child, you couldn't hardly remember that far back and that never happened anyway," Madeline said. "Look who can't handle her alcohol. You're drunk—and delusional."

"Mother, I might be drunk and at times I might be delusional," Ginger said. "This ain't one of those times. I recall clearly being hungry and scared and wondering where you were. Daddy used to kiss me goodbye; he was working the third or fourth shift at night. I was at home with you and you would leave me, make me go to bed and I'd lay there and cry and you would leave anyway."

"Ginger, that just did not happen," Madeline insisted. "I might have left you and went outside for a few minutes. But that's it. If you were crying it wasn't because of me. I was there for you."

Ginger took a deep breath. Her tone lowered, but her words were figuratively booming.

"Were you there when Uncle Ambrose came into my room that night you left me and went to the card game next door?" Ginger asked.

Whatever buzz Madeline had evaporated immediately. "What? What are you talking about, Ginger?"

"You heard me," her daughter responded.

Paul was shocked and concerned, too. He had not heard this from his wife, and when they were right, they talked about every-thing. At least, that's what he thought.

"Ginger, please don't tell me he did something to you," Madeline said. She was almost crying. "Please don't tell me that."

"It was a Friday night," Ginger said.

"Gin," Paul said, the concern in his voice evident.

"It's OK," she said. "I was in bed, waiting for you to come check on me, but you never did. So I finally fell asleep, but I woke up when I felt my bed move. I jumped up. I was so scared. It was Uncle Ambrose. He said, 'Hey, baby. I didn't mean to scare you. I came in here to tuck you in, make sure you're all right.'

"His voice sounded strange, like he was someone else.

I was only five years old but right away I realized something was wrong. But I didn't know what to say.

"So, he slid closer to me; he was sitting at the foot of my bed at first. Then I knew something was really wrong because he pulled my covers back. I was confused. 'If he's trying to tuck me in, why is he taking the covers off me?' My little five-year-old brain could process that something was wrong.

"I could smell the alcohol on his breath; he was reeking. He put his hand on my shoulder. He said something like, 'Kiss your Uncle Ambrose good night.' Then he tapped his lips. 'Here. Kiss your Uncle Ambrose good night right here.'

"Now I was really scared. But before I could scream, Daddy came in the room. He grabbed Uncle Ambrose and threw him on the floor. He came over to me and asked me if I was OK. I couldn't talk; I nodded my head. He leaned over and hugged me and kissed me on my face and pulled the covers back over top of me.

"He said, 'Go to sleep, baby. I will be back to check on you later. Sweet dreams.' Then he pulled Uncle Ambrose up off the floor and dragged him out of the room....I never saw Uncle Ambrose again."

Madeline had a look of shock on her face. For several seconds, she did not say anything. Paul and Brenda were riveted to Ginger's words and did not know what to say. Finally, Madeline broke her silence.

"It all makes sense now," she said. "I know exactly the night you are speaking of, baby. That was the night your uncle was found not far from our house, beaten almost to death. No one ever knew what happened to him.

"The last person to see him was one of our neighbors who said he swore he saw Ambrose go into our house that night. And he saw your father go into the house a little while later. But he never saw Ambrose come out. The police questioned us—everyone who was next door at the card game, the neighbors—and according to them, that was the last time he was seen in a healthy condition, walking into the front door of our house."

"What do you mean, it makes sense now, Momma?" Ginger asked.

"I'm so sorry," she said.

"For what, Momma?"

"I left you alone and my brother would have probably raped you if your father hadn't come home when he did," Madeline said. "Ambrose was sick; he wasn't playing with a full deck. There were times when everyone was afraid of him. He was liable to do anything. But your father told me—and I'll never forget his words—he said: 'Maddy, if he puts a hand on you or Ginger I swear to you I will kill him.'

"Your father had never spoken to me with such force and conviction about anything. I knew he meant it."

"What are you saying? That Daddy killed Uncle Ambrose?"

Madeline looked away, toward the mountains that sandwiched Interstate 80.

"Mother," Ginger pleaded.

"He didn't technically kill him," Madeline said, turning to her daughter. "When Ambrose was found, he was alive, but really in bad shape. He was in the hospital for several days and then one day had a heart attack and died. So, that's what was on his death certificate. The doctors couldn't tell if the beating he took played a role in his death.

"But all makes sense now. That night, when I finally saw your father, he was sweating and exhausted and acting weird, like something was bothering him. For the longest time, he seemed different. You didn't know Ambrose died because your father told me not to tell you. He said you were too young and you didn't need to know about death at such a young age.

"I went along with it because he was my husband and it wasn't an outrageous request. Richard was very solemn at the funeral, but not sad, if you know what I mean. He seemed down, but not sad that Ambrose was dead. He was carrying a heavy burden. I always felt it but now I realize that he had beaten my brother to the brink of death.

"And he was sitting there through his funeral listening to people get up there and talk about how much they loved him and how much of a good man he was. He was my brother and I did love him; we grew up in the same house. But Ambrose had some issues. He functioned OK and worked, but we used to say in the family that we wouldn't be surprised if he ended up being anything from a bank robber to a serial killer."

"Oh, my God," Ginger said. "You're saying Daddy killed a man?"

"Again, he died of a heart attack," Madeline said. "But the guy who lived next door saw Richard go in the house after Ambrose, but he didn't see either of them come out of the house. That's because Richard took him out of the back. He was found less than a mile from our house—the back of our house.

"And I was there when Richard came home—he came in through the back door. And, based on the police report, he came home long after the guy saw Richard go into the front door of the house."

"I can't even believe this," Ginger said. "I mean, I am glad my father protected me when I needed protecting. But…"

"I'm blown away, too," Madeline said. "Richard never said anything to me about him touching you or being in your room. But he didn't because he knew I would have dug up Ambrose's body and killed him again. Oh, my God."

"There goes my little high," Brenda said. "This is deep."

"Ginger, you OK?" Paul asked.

"I don't know," she said. "I mean, I'm OK. But I don't know. I know my father as one thing and now I learn he almost murdered my uncle."

"But—wait, excuse me," Brenda said. "I don't mean to be all in this but I'm right here and couldn't help but hear everything. Is it OK if I ask something?"

Madeline and Ginger both said it was OK.

"How can you not know what you feel about this?" Brenda said. "Your father protected you. He swore that he would end the person's life that laid a hand on you. This guy did and he probably led to his dying because— if what Madeline says is true—he would have been back, and maybe trying to hurt you.

"I'm not very comfortable saying this, but he got what he deserved and your daddy should be a bigger hero in your eyes than he ever was. I'm not condoning killing, but you were a five-year-old girl. What if your father hadn't come home? How many other girls had he touched and done God-knows-what to?

"I'm sorry; that's my two cents."

"It does mean a lot to me that he saved me from something that could have scarred me for life. But…"

"Ginger," Madeline said, "there are no buts. What's the word? Romanticize? I'm not trying to romanticize what Richard did. But there are millions of fathers who say they would have done the same thing. Richard, I believe, did it."

"Gin," Paul said, "if someone, anyone, put a hand on you or Helena in that way, I would kill him, too. Actually doing it is one thing. But that's what I believe. Your dad protected you. I respect him even more now than I already did."

"I wish I could call and ask him what happened," Ginger said. "I want to hear him say it to believe it."

"Well, unless you want to have a séance, that's not going to happen," Madeline said.

"I think," Paul said, "you should let it go. In the scheme

of things, something that happened that long ago should not matter much now."

"I don't know about that," Ginger said. "I mean, it happened, so how can it not matter?"

Brenda said, "Everything that happens doesn't matter. And if you ignore it, it's like it didn't happen."

"You spit some knowledge, Ma," Paul said.

"'Spit some knowledge?'" Ginger asked. "Who are you?"

"Don't be mad that I am in tune with the ways of the youth," Paul said.

"*Please*. You're not in tune with the ways of the middle-aged," Ginger said, laughing.

Paul had successfully moved Ginger off her base of lamenting the possibility of her father's actions. And he was intent on keeping her away from that subject.

"OK, copilot, where do we exit?" he said, handing her back her cell phone.

Ginger gave Paul the specifics and looked out of the window at the mountainside they passed. It was quiet in the car for several minutes, with all the ladies dozing off, one-by-one.

That was a relief for Paul, who did not give the demands of traveling with three women much thought when he cooked up the idea. He was focused on reconnecting with his wife and wine. As he swerved into the valley, his mind wandered.

It was gnawing at him that he had not told Ginger of their newfound wealth. He felt a lot better about where they were going in the marriage, and that she was receptive to making it work after so much bad stuff.

Paul purchased a David Yurman diamond ring for Ginger, a gift he planned to give to her on the trip, after he was sure she was sincere about making the marriage work. He figured the last vineyard they would visit would be Sterling in Calistoga, where they would take a tram up to the top of the mountain to visit the winery.

Its website indicated and the pictures confirmed it was one of the most romantic wineries in Napa Valley, with pristine views of beauty stretching miles and miles in every direction. Out on the deck was where he envisioned presenting it to Ginger, a gift to consummate a restart of their marriage. He would tell them later, at the hotel about the money. That was his plan.

He drove past signs saying Vallejo and continued along dark stretches where he, at times, could see beautiful landscape. He let the window down for a minute to consume the breeze and the smell of fresh California air.

Paul felt more carefree than he ever had. He was on his dream trip with his dream girl and, while the trip promised some bumpy times, he anticipated the sense of family to come out of it would be worth the occasional discord.

He hoped.

CHAPTER 8
HOTEL, MOTEL, HOLIDAY INN

As if they could sense they were getting close to the hotel, the ladies all woke up within minutes of each other. Paul was glad they were close because he had to go to the bathroom for the previous twenty-five miles, but did not want to stop or disturb the sleeping women.

"How close are we now, Vino?" Brenda said. It was the first time she used her nickname for her son around Madeline.

"Vino? Who's Vino?" Madeline asked.

"I am," Paul answered. "It's my mom's pet name for me, so to speak."

"I know the next question," Brenda said. "The answer is, I was with him the night he discovered that he liked wine. It was amazing. He was like a self-taught expert, right from the start. He could taste the elements of the wine and tell you what it was. Accurately. He was amazing.

"And he was twenty-one. How many young men at that age are even *trying* wine? Well, Paul was. He was drinking it and loving it and analyzing it.

"So, one day I called him 'Wino,' and he was offended.

He said, 'A wino doesn't appreciate wine. He only appreciates the next drink he can get.'

"Of course, I let that nickname go right away because he was right. So I decided on 'Vino.' Wine. If there were a word for wine lover, I would call him that. Since there isn't, I just call him 'Vino.' It fits. He's all about wine."

"All right now," Madeline said. "Vino, get us to the Marriott, please."

"You know what's crazy, Mrs. Wall?" Ginger said. "He loves wines so much and studied them. And yet, he won't do anything with this knowledge.

"I told him to go be a bartender at a wine bar. Become a sommelier."

"A what?" Ginger's mom said.

"A sommelier," Ginger answered. "A sommelier is a wine expert, someone who can pair wines with meals based on understanding wine. They know everything about wines.

"When he lost his job, there was the perfect opportunity to pursue his passion," Ginger said. "But he did nothing."

"I didn't not do anything," Paul said. "I did a lot of stuff. I just didn't do anything with wine."

"Except drink it," his mom chipped in.

It was an uncomfortable subject for Paul. Even though his life had changed with winning the lottery, losing his job scarred him. His manhood was stripped, and it affected his marriage.

"You know, life is full of surprises," he said. "Maybe I

will take on something working with wines. It's never too late."

He said it so convincingly that he believed it. And then his mind started roaming. He now had the resources to do whatever he liked. He did not want to be a bartender because he did not want to serve others in that way. But he did like the idea of talking to people about wine. In just a few minutes of contemplation, he conceived of opening a wine store where he picked the wines and could host wine-tastings each month and share his knowledge.

He hadn't thought much about what to do with all that money, except save it, travel and buy wine. He told himself he would share his thoughts with the ladies before they departed.

They were all up and alert by the time he pulled up at the Napa Marriott. There were some lavish hotels in Napa that Paul wanted to experience, but they were so pricey that Ginger would have questioned why he would spend so much money.

Besides, the Marriott was nice and convenient and it served a Thanksgiving dinner, too.

Paul emptied the trunk of their luggage-on-wheels and everyone pulled their bags into the lobby, which was buzzing with people at the bar and dining in the restaurant.

When he got the room keys, a sudden fear came over him: how are the in-laws going to get along sharing a room? He made sure his and Ginger's parents were on the same floor, but down the hall from their room.

"What time is dinner?" Brenda said. "Do I have time for a nap?"

"It's at eight-thirty, but we can push it back if we need to," Paul said. "I talked to the host. The evening is open in the restaurant. And they are serving dinner until eleven."

He handed the ladies the keys and they made their way to their rooms. As Paul and Ginger headed to their room, Ginger surprised him. "What room am I in?" she asked.

"Don't even play with me, Gin," Paul said.

"I'm not playing. Who said we were going to stay in the same room?" she said.

"I did," Paul answered. He had arrived at the door to the room and slid in the card key.

"You coming in?" he said, holding the door open.

Ginger just looked at him.

"Gin, we're all the way here now and you don't want to stay in the same room with your husband?" Paul said. "Come on. That's not cool."

"It's not about cool," Ginger said. "We have problems."

"We can't work them out here in the hallway, Ginger," he said.

That bit of reasoning worked, and she entered the room, which was nothing special. But it did have two double beds, which she acknowledged.

"This is my bed," she said.

Paul ignored her, but placed his carry-on on the other bed. He zipped open his other bag and fumbled through it until he pulled out a bottle of Fairview Pinotage, a South

African wine given to him as a gift by a former coworker who visited the vineyard in the summer.

"I have been waiting to crack this," Paul said. "This is the time."

Ginger's sudden discomfort could not mask her desire to share the wine. She enjoyed it—probably not as much as Paul, but she could have at least a glass almost every day.

This was a special bottle that Paul coveted, so she was moved that he brought it to share with her. But she was still damaged by his behavior over the previous several months.

Ginger realized she was sending him mixed signals, but that's what was coming out of heart and her head. They clashed.

"Be right back," Paul said. "Gonna get some wine-glasses from the bar."

He made his way to the bar and was shocked by what he saw: his mother and mother-in-law sitting in the lounge together sipping wine. Paul quickly turned away and acted as if he did not see them. He did not want to interrupt their moment and he wanted to get back to Ginger.

Inhaling the Napa Valley air did something to Paul. He could smell the grapes in the air, although it was not prime grape-growing season. Still, being there and passing the vineyards on the way in improved his already-uplifted spirits and made him frisky and romantic. He wanted his wife back.

When he returned with the glasses, Ginger was in the

bathroom, which gave Paul time to dig into his luggage and pull out a scented candle. He lit it and pulled open the drapes, which revealed a swimming pool.

He wiped down the glasses, but did not open the wine until Ginger came out. He wanted her to share in that moment. That's how seriously he took wine—opening a bottle was important.

"What's this?" Ginger said when she reentered the room. The candle made it cozy and romantic. She had not seen that kind of thing from Paul in at least a decade.

"It's a nice mood for us to enjoy this great wine," he said.

Ginger did not respond or resist. Her husband gave her a glass and he sat next to her on "her" bed. He cracked open the bottle. "I waited for you to be here to open it," he said.

She smiled. After pouring each a glass, Paul lifted his and proposed a toast: "To my wife. I am thankful that you are here with me in the one place I really wanted to visit. And to be here now, on Thanksgiving, really brings it all together because I am really thankful that you are my wife."

Ginger smiled. She was touched. She tapped her glass into his and they both smelled the wine, then swirled it around in their glasses, sniffed it again to see the difference from the oxidation and then took a sip.

"Oh, man," Paul said, a smile developing on his face. "What do you think?"

Ginger smiled, too. "Excellent," she said. "There is no aftertaste in this wine."

"And it is smoky with dark fruit flavors," Earl said. "Wanna hear some history on Pinotage? Remember, I studied it."

"Sure, why not? What else do I have to do?" Ginger said.

"Keep sippin' while I kick the knowledge," Paul said.

"Kick the knowledge?" Ginger said, shaking her head. "Anyway, go ahead."

"Pinotage is a unique South African grape variety that only grows well in South Africa," Paul explained. "Most wine drinkers have less experience with it than other red wines. And guess what: Some South Africans love it, but some don't like it so much because it is not European enough. It does not possess any of the flavors of French wines.

"The Pinotage grape is a combination of a Pinot Noir grape and Hermitage grape that was created in 1925 and is one of the younger red wines Thus, Pinotage. Last thing: They actually grow Pinotage in a few places in California and Virginia."

"Interesting," Ginger said. "You really should do something with all this knowledge. I mean, I've been thinking about it. With all the layoffs in the last years, many people have decided to pursue their passion, to do what they really want to do. I realize you like heating and air conditioning repair. But you love wine, Paul."

That confirmed Paul's earlier thoughts.

"I do, and I'm really surprised you said that because I actually have been thinking the same thing," he said. "Maybe, in time, we could open up a wine store and host wine-tastings. Make it really nice. Educate people."

"That sounds nice, Paul, but that costs money," Ginger said.

Paul poured more wine in her glass. "Well, you never know. Things could turn around for us. They *will* turn around for us. And when they do, that's something we can explore. I'd like you to be my partner."

"That's a long way off," Ginger said. "A long way."

"Maybe. Maybe not," Paul said, smiling. "You have to put it out in the universe for it to become reality... But I'd rather talk about us."

"What about us?" Ginger said.

"Well, we've made some progress since we hit rock bottom—since I hit rock bottom," he said. "I think we have. We are talking. We made love. We are here in California. Two months ago, I wouldn't have expected any of this."

"Me, either, and that's why I'm trying to figure out what changed," Ginger said.

"I changed," Paul said. "I got off my ass and finally stopped feeling sorry for myself and realized nothing happens unless I make it happen."

"And that's it?" she asked.

"No," he said. Paul sipped more wine and shook his

head. "No. When I took inventory, I realized that I was ruining our marriage. You're not perfect and neither am I. But you're perfect for me. I believe that."

Ginger's head was spinning. Literally. The wine took hold and Paul's words did, too. And so, when Paul slid beside her on the bed, she did not resist. He went for it.

"I love you, Gin," he said. "I will apologize every day if I have to, to get you to understand how badly I feel about the things I said. And I will kiss you right here on your neck every day, too. You like me to kiss you right there, don't you?"

Ginger did not want to answer, but her body was all his now, as if all the months of trouble and pain and concerns did not happen. Anger, disappointment, sadness…none of that mattered in that moment. When her body spoke, she listened and acquiesced to its needs.

Paul knew this, and he turned his wife's face toward his with a gentle tug. She was breathless. Between the wine and the signals her brain sent through her body—and the love she tried to suppress for Paul—she was defenseless. He kissed her on her lips, which were moist with anticipation.

His lips were thick and soft, and they met hers as two wine-glasses would meet to climax an intimate toast. Ginger closed her eyes and Paul closed his, and they delighted in a deep, passionate kiss that made Ginger woozy when their lips finally parted.

The small portion of her brain that was not covered

in passion tried to resist. She stood up to catch her breath, but Paul stood up, too, to restrict her breathing by kissing her again as he wrapped his arms firmly around her.

Paul's heart beat as if he had been sprinting. It was the combination of unmitigated passion with his wife and the intensity of the kiss that heightened his desires. And so, he leaned away from Ginger and, while looking into her eyes, slowly unbuttoned the front of her shirt.

As each button came loose, Ginger breathed in, until Paul got to the end and slowly pulled off the blouse and discarded it like a piece of tissue into a wastebasket. Ginger stood there, staring at her man, feeling like she did when they first met, when they had sex as if their survival depended upon it.

That was such a joyous time in their lives, and to feel like that made Ginger finally release any inhibitions and meet Paul's desires with her own passion.

So as Paul fumbled slightly with unhitching her bra, Ginger politely took his hands and placed them over her firm breasts and she reached behind her back and released the strap in an instant. Paul knew his wife, and that maneuver meant the resistance was over. They could not dance to their rhythm.

Since winning the lottery and regaining some self-esteem, Paul dropped significant weight, making him look more like the man she married than the man she loathed. He had only had sex with his wife once in the previous two months, and she had not seen his new body in the flesh.

Paul, eager to show it off, pulled his shirt over his head and stood in front of his panting wife as if to say, "This is all yours. What you gonna do with it?"

Ginger read her husband's look and she slowly, seductively unbuckled and unzipped her pants, never taking her eyes off Paul's, who was unbuckling and unzipping his pants, too. When their underwear dropped to the floor, it was like the starter's gun to a race went off.

They attacked each other, kissing and groping in a furious fashion that somehow was in rhythm, a seductive dance that extended from one side of a queen-sized bed to the other.

Finally, the foreplay turned into lovemaking that they had not experienced in years. About two months before the trip they had a sexual encounter that was more about them having a need than having sex. This was passion. This was intense.

Ginger allowed Paul to lead the family, but she, at times, liked to be in charge of certain situations. Intimacy with him was one of them. She liked to be on top so she could control the passion: How deep Paul entered her, how rapid the thrusts, the angle of penetration.

All Paul had to do was hold on. Ginger was at her dick-riding best, squirming her saturated vagina on his hardness in swift counterclockwise rotations, which allowed for pleasure along multiple areas of her inner walls.

Paul tried to thrust upward, but Ginger's pace was fast and did not allow much for his participation. She rocked her hips and enjoyed his joystick with abashed pleasure. The wine made her feel uninhibited, and her actions spoke the truth about how she felt.

She kissed Paul deeply as she changed her sexual attack. Now she bounced up and down on his manhood. Paul stroked upward to her cadence, creating a smacking sound as they challenged each other on how deep he could get and how much she could take.

Well, she took everything he had to offer and he offered a lot. He held her by her waist and pulled her down to meet his thrusts, making it almost a violent collision of passion. Ginger moaned with each thumping, but there were moans of pleasure and pain coming together as only can happen in intense sex.

Paul grunted with each thrust, an indication of how intent he was on getting deeper and making sure his wife felt his intent. After two minutes of straight pounding each other, Paul began to sweat, and immediately he went back to their early sexual sessions that really solidified their bond.

Those experiences were few and far between over the years, but in that moment of feeling sweat develop on his forehead and slide down his face, he made a commitment to return their sex lives back to something sensual and passionate, romantic and lasting.

Losing his job diminished his sex drive, and he was

embarrassed at the weak effort he gave Ginger in the first weeks after being laid off. Sex became less important because his manhood was threatened with being out of work. His erections were mild, or certainly unlike the pole-hard stiffness he banged Ginger with their first hours in Napa Valley.

Ginger noticed the difference—in how he handled her and the strength of his hardness. She might have been in control of the movements while being on top, but Paul was in control of the pleasure.

Ultimately, he won out on that battle; his forcefulness was unrelenting. He was too proud to let Ginger wear him out, and so he kept feeding her until she exploded in herky-jerky body gyrations and weird sounds that had only one interpretation: ecstasy.

Her movements were so wild that all Paul could do was hold on until she gathered herself, which took another minute or so. It was then when he flipped her onto her back and began his pleasure quest by holding up her legs and spreading them as he threw his head back and pumped deeper and deeper into her.

She took his strokes with sounds of pleasure, and Paul felt like he was having an out-of-body experience. He and Ginger had not enjoyed that kind of relentless passion in some time, so long that he could not even recall.

And when he looked down and saw the pleasure on his wife's face—a look he had not put there in months— he became so excited that he stroked her harder and harder, generating a sensation that ran through his body and exploded out of the head of his penis and into Ginger's waiting canal.

It was his turn to yell something incoherent but translated into the ultimate pleasure. He collapsed his much larger body onto Ginger's and she took him without issue, hugging him firmly as he breathed heavily over her shoulder.

"My God," Paul managed to get out after a few minutes. "I forgot how incredible we can be together."

"It has been a long time," she said.

Paul realized he was suffocating her, so he rolled over, and they both let out a sigh.

"This is how it should be all the time," Paul said. He held her hand and turned toward her. "I messed things up, but I want us to get back to where we were. And I also realize it will take time. But I hope this is the start of us getting back to where we were when we were happy."

Ginger's cautious side wanted to offer something negative, or at least something that would not indicate she was all in. And that made her mad. *Why can't I embrace what was good without second-guessing?* she wondered.

It was her nature to find the cracks and pounce on them. This time, though, her body told her to cut it out, to let go. She loved her husband and he had just put it on her in a display of passion and love that she missed— and needed.

That was the key. Ginger had girlfriends who insisted they did not need a man and could get by without sex in their lives. She did not understand that. She needed the physical aspect of lovemaking in her life and she needed the emotional connection that came with it. She wanted to believe she could have one without the other, but she could not convince herself of that.

She felt most emotionally connected to Paul when they consistently had sex. It was not the elixir to all things broken. But it was the foundation of holding things together.

So when Paul's sex drive diminished with his loss of self-esteem, their connection to each other slowly dwindled, too. Laying on her back after a vigorous round of passion with Paul made Ginger feel alive.

"I want the same thing, Paul," she said. "I do. But I'm scared. I'm scared because I don't know what brought you around and if you'll go back to that place where you were depressed and cold and sometimes just mean to me.

"It has been a very rough last year or so with you. I felt like my family was falling apart. Thank God we were able to somehow shield our troubles from Helena.

"You don't know this, but I have gone through a lot because of this. It has been a very difficult time. And I couldn't even talk to you about it because we were so fractured. Still, I believed it was a phase. I never expected to hear you say you wanted a divorce. That was very hurtful and it put me in a really bad place. I don't know. I am here, in Napa, because I want to save our marriage. And as great as it has been so far, I can't get out of my head how things have been."

"I understand," Paul said. "I do. But I was going through

something that I did not know how to handle. They say you lash out at the people you are closest to when you're under duress. Well, I was under duress. I worked all my life. I provided for my family from Day One.

"To be let go after so many years and so much commitment to the job, it crushed me. And I won't even try to lie: My ego was crushed, too. We probably should have sought counseling then. Maybe it would have helped if I opened up. But I can't even say now, looking back on it, that I would have said the things necessary to heal.

"I felt sorry for myself and nothing was going to get me out of that mode until I found a job. I need to provide for my family."

"But Paul, it's not like we were going to lose our house. We saved well enough to survive for a while. And you should have known that providing for your family means more than money. You weren't the only one going through something. I needed you to be there for me, and you weren't. You were in your own world.

"Our daughter needed you to attend her events and really be more a part of her last year of high school. You were at her graduation and you were great. But leading up to that, you were not pleasant to be around."

Paul lifted his wife's hand toward his face, leaned over and kissed it.

"You haven't kissed my hand in more than a year," Ginger said. "It might sound crazy to you, but you kissed my hand at the end of our first date. I was expecting a kiss—we had such a nice time—at least on the cheek. But at my door you told me you were glad we met, reached down and pulled up my hand and gently kissed it.

"And that was so damn erotic and sexy and gentlemanly. I was turned on. From there, every so often you would kiss my hand when I was upset or when you wanted sex or when you were just being nice. I have missed that."

Paul wanted to tell his wife at that moment about the lottery money, that their lives had changed forever, that they could do whatever they wanted without regard for finances. But he didn't. He listened to the doubts she expressed and decided to hold on to his secret a little while longer, when Ginger seemed all in and doubt-free.

Instead, he said, "I don't know about you, but I'm starting over. I'm rebuilding. I'm committed to making the effort to regain your trust and full commitment to the marriage. I understand your feelings, but I'm going to do what I need to do, what I'm supposed to do, to make things right."

"Well, that sounds good to me, Paul," Ginger said. "I guess we'll just have to see."

Paul pulled her closer to him and she rested her head on his chest. "We have about an hour, maybe ninety minutes before dinner. Let's get a quick nap and have a great Thanksgiving dinner," he said.

"I wonder how our mothers are getting along," Ginger said.

"I wonder, too," Paul said.

CHAPTER 9
MOMMA MIA

T he mothers spent their time before Thanksgiving dinner enhancing their buzz with glass after glass of Cabernet Sauvignon.

"I needed this time away more than those kids of ours needed it," Madeline said. "They have their neat little lives, daughter off to college. And here we are. I'm a widow and you're divorced."

"But we can't let that keep us down," Brenda said. "I had my moments of depression, even though I was the one who wanted a divorce. But I got over it."

"How?" Madeline wanted to know. "How did you do it because it's been almost ten months since my husband died. And I feel strange even thinking about another man."

"You gotta believe you don't need another man to get on with your life," Brenda said. "I said you gotta believe that shit—but you don't have to deny yourself, either."

The women laughed and Madeline said, "I *know* that's right."

"Girl, I got on the Internet and joined a dating service and I have met two really nice men," Brenda said. "Please don't tell Paul this. He thinks he's my protector. He bought me the computer and told me to not even think about those dating sites because—how did he put it?—they attract 'the man who is not interested in nothing but having sex. They figure that you are desperate to be on a dating site, then you will be easy to get in bed. I'm not trying to hear about you being stalked—or worse—by someone you met online,' he said.

"I let him live his life, you know? He's got to let me live mine. You can believe his father is living his."

"Well, truth be told," Madeline said, "I did meet someone. He was visiting my church. Retired military. He lives in San Diego. Retired there. Said he would be in Sacramento visiting his cousin or some relative while we are here. So I might have to sneak away for a day to see him. I like him. Charming. Smart. We've had dinner and breakfast together."

"On the same date?" Brenda asked.

Madeline looked embarrassed. "What can I say?" she answered.

"Listen at you," Brenda said. "You should tell him to bring a friend and we can double date. Shoot, I ain't above no blind date."

"You know what? That's a good idea," Madeline said. "Where's my phone? I don't know how to text that well; Ginger showed me how. But that's the way the young folks do it. They send a text. I'm not trying to be that young, but I don't want to seem that old, either."

The combination of the wine impacting her coordination and the touch screen to her iPhone made it an adventure for her to complete the text. "Shoot, I guess we can have another glass of wine while you figure that whole thing out," Brenda said.

After nearly five minutes, she was done. "Damn, I'm exhausted," Madeline said. "Next time, I'm just calling. Trying to act young is too exhausting for me. And I only typed three sentences."

"I ain't that hip myself, but I know you have to abbreviate," Brenda said. "I'm glad you at least tried. You're so prim and proper."

"I might be prim and proper," Madeline said. "But I can get down and dirty when I need to. But ladies rarely go there."

"You trying to say something about me?" Brenda asked, smiling.

"Of course, not," Madeline said.

Before Brenda could reply, she looked up to see Paul and Ginger approaching. She looked at her watch. It was Thanksgiving dinnertime.

"I can't believe you are down here before us," Ginger said.

"Honey, they have been here since we got here," Paul said.

The mothers looked at Paul in a strange way.

"That's right, isn't it?" he asked. "I saw you all when I came down here to get some wineglasses. That was almost two hours ago."

"Mother, you have been drinking wine all that time?" Ginger asked.

"Not all that time," Madeline answered. "But most of it."

And she and Brenda burst out laughing, loudly. Ginger and Paul looked at each other. They were in for an interesting evening.

"I thought you wanted to shower and change clothes, Mother," Ginger said.

"I decided to sit here with Brenda and enjoy life instead," her mom said. "I'll do that later. And I know one thing: I'm hungry. Wine does three things for me: makes me hungry, makes me feel good, and makes me want to wee-wee."

"That's too much information, Maddy," Brenda said. "Yes, that's my new nickname for you. Maddy. Madeline has too many syllables."

"Oh, boy," Paul said. "They are both tipsy as hell."

"Vino, it's OK," Brenda said as she pulled herself from her seat. "We're fine. You know what, son? This was a great idea. I am so glad to be here. And you're right: Maddy isn't the bitch I thought she was."

"OK, OK," Paul said to his mother. "Maybe you should have some water."

"We're going to the bathroom; come on, Maddy," Brenda said. "Get us a table for dinner, Paul. We'll be right back."

The moms composed themselves and walked arm-in-arm to the restroom.

Ginger turned to Paul. "You called my mother a bitch?"

"What? No," Paul said. "Come on, now. I love your mother, even if she has issues with me. And why would I say something like that? My mom didn't even say that. She said she didn't believe she could get along with your mother. And I told her your mom wasn't as bad as she thought."

"That's not the same as saying you love her, Paul," Ginger said.

"It ain't calling her a bitch, either," he said. "Hold up. Are you trying to start a fight? After what we just did and what we just shared? I told you neither of us called your mom a bitch. My mom obviously is feeling the wine. So whatever comes out of her mouth is suspect."

"Or the truth," Ginger said. "You know what they say: A drunk person speaks a sober man's thoughts."

"Yeah, well, I'm focusing on the good thing and that's that they are getting along," Paul said. "I hoped for this but didn't expect it."

"Well, that's true," Ginger said. "I guess we should ride this wave as long as we can."

"That's right because even the biggest wave reaches shore and dies at some point," Paul said.

"Let's get some wine and drink to them being BFFs for now," Ginger said.

They went to the reception area and were seated near a fireplace. He held the chair for Ginger and placed her cloth napkin in her lap.

"Look who's suddenly Mr. Chivalry now," she joked. "I guess good sex brings out all kinds of stuff."

"Especially good sex after not having any for about a year," Paul said.

"Excuse me, but we had sex about two months ago and two months before that," Ginger asserted.

"That's a pretty sad timeline. But it wasn't anything like what just happened," Paul said. "We had sex then. Just now, we had *sex* and we made love at the same time. Know what I'm saying?"

Ginger blushed.

Their parents arrived at that table about that time. They had killed a bottle and a half by themselves and it was obvious. They were as giddy as schoolgirls, laughing and joking as if they were life-long pals.

Ginger and Paul were amazed.

Everyone ordered the holiday dinner of turkey, dressing, yams and greens and enjoyed it to the hilt, all the while engaging in lighthearted conversation that made it feel like a family meal.

Madeline and Brenda passed on wine with their meals, but they allowed Paul to order a bottle as a nightcap, Shiraz, and when all was poured in the glasses, he offered a toast.

"This is what family is about—enjoying each other and loving life. I've always wanted this for us, so if feels good to finally have it."

They tapped glasses and, for Paul, he felt on top of his world. He was healthy, his wife seemed to be coming around and he was a millionaire. He felt the urge to tell the ladies of his luck, but thought better of it. *Not yet*, he said to himself.

"Look at you two," Brenda said, staring at her son and Ginger. "Y'all look like you just had sex."

Paul practically choked on his wine.

"You know what? You're right," Madeline chimed in. "Look at you, Ginger. I noticed it when you first came down, but I let it go. You all been up there doing the do."

"Mother," Ginger said. "I don't believe you. Doing the do?"

"Yes, but am I wrong?" Madeline asked.

"If you were right or wrong, I wouldn't answer," Ginger said. "I can't believe you would even ask me something like that." Brenda said. "Paul's just a smiling. I recognize the look. He ain't said a word."

"'Cause he doesn't have a thing to say about that," Paul said. "This is a case when too much good wine goes wrong."

"Can we get back to the meal?" Ginger said.

"Why isn't Helena with us?" Madeline asked. "It would be perfect if she was here, too."

"I know," Brenda said. "I don't get to see my grand-daughter enough as it is."

"Who's fault, is that, Ma?" Paul said. "Helena wanted to go to her roommate's home and spend the holiday there. She's loving her college experience and sometimes that's a part of it. She'll be home for Christmas.

"And this is a grown people trip. Would you be drinking as much wine as you have if she were here?"

"Yes, I would, because I'm grown and can do whatever I want to do," Brenda said. "And the reason I say she should be here is because I remember what it was like for me when I went to my roommate's hometown for a weekend in college."

"Well," Ginger said, "Miss Wall, we spoke to the young lady's parents and they are aware that they are teenagers who are young and can get wild. I'm not stupid: Helena isn't an angel, at least not around us.

"I spoke to her earlier and she said she is fine and enjoying herself. It's a parent's nature to worry. But I'm not going to drive myself crazy with it by making sure she's with us all the time. She needs her freedom to build responsibility."

"Yes, but this is family time and she should be with her family," Madeline said.

Ginger resisted the urge to snap at her mom, and instead reached for the wine. "Well, in reality, it was our decision, Mother," she said.

"I've never seen you sip so much wine," Paul quickly added, attempting to advance the conversation.

"I never *needed* to sip so much wine," Ginger said.

Paul smiled, but no one else did. He looked at his mother and the look on her face was not a good one.

"Ma, what's wrong?" he asked.

"I don't feel good," she said. "Too much wine."

"I don't feel good, either," Madeline said.

"Mother, what's wrong?" Ginger asked.

"My head. My stomach," she answered.

"What kind of wine were you drinking?" Paul said. "Both of you not feeling good? This is crazy."

"I'm feeling sick," Brenda said. She pushed away from table and placed both her hands over her stomach. Her face became flushed, her skin clammy.

"Come on, let's go to the bathroom," Paul said.

"I'm going, too," Madeline said. "I'm going to throw up."

Ginger and Paul hurried from the table and helped usher the women toward the bathroom.

"Ma, wine doesn't do this to you," Paul said. "I don't understand this."

Three feet from the bathroom door, Brenda threw up, a heaping splattering of her breakfast, lunch, dinner and drinks. Seeing that helped Madeline throw up, too.

And passersby shook their heads in disgust. Paul and Ginger went straight to caregiver roles, trying to comfort their moms.

"I got them," Ginger said, as she walked the ladies into the bathroom. She glanced down at the vomit on the floor. "Maybe you should get that up," she said to Paul.

"Hell, no," he said. "I'll get some paper towels and cover it, but that's it."

And so he did and then went back to the table to finish the wine, pay the bill and wait on the ladies. After about fifteen minutes, they came out, and he rushed from the restaurant area to meet them.

"You feeling better?" he said to his mom, as he clutched her arm.

"I feel woozy, but a little better," she said. "Seems like I've got to get whatever's left in my stomach out of it."

"I don't understand," Paul said. "For both of you to have a reaction like this over wine doesn't seem right."

No one responded to Paul, which made him uneasy, curious. They continued toward the elevator without anyone saying anything.

Finally, as they got into the elevator, the mothers looking totally worn down and intoxicated, Ginger let it out.

"They got sick because your mother ordered shots," Ginger said with anger in her voice.

"Shots?" Paul said. "Shots of what?"

"Tequila."

"Ma, you don't even like tequila," he said. "Why would you do that?"

"I don't know and I'm too sick to go into it now," she said, her voice weary.

Ginger looked at Paul with fire in her eyes. He looked at his mother with dismay as he helped her into her room. She collapsed on the queen-sized bed closest to the bathroom.

"Paul, I feel like I'm going to throw up again," Brenda said. "I need you to stay here and take care of me."

He did not know what to do, so Ginger spoke up.

"Yeah, he can stay here with you and I will take Mother to our room," she said.

Paul's head snapped in her direction. In his mind the night would be spent resuming their lovemaking of earlier in the day. Ginger knew what was on his mind.

"That's right," she said. "You stay here with your mother since she created this…situation."

She and Madeline headed out the door toward Paul's and Ginger's room.

"You're blaming this on my mother?" Paul said. "Last I looked your mother is a grown woman and I'm sure no one made her drink that tequila."

Ginger said, "My mother ordered the second shot, but your mom shouldn't have even brought tequila into the equation."

"Oh, she did?" Paul said, looking side-eyed at Ginger, who was standing in the doorway with her mother on her arm. "I guess I should be mad at your mom, huh?"

Ginger turned and slowly walked three rooms down the hallway with her mother. There, she was glad they had two beds because she and Paul had littered the other bed, closest to the window, in their passion.

Her mom said, "Let me lay down for a few," she said. "I feel so weak and so…so drunk. I need to close my eyes and get my head together and my stomach right."

Ginger took off her shoes. "I'll be right back," she said. "I'm going to get a gown from your room so you can change."

In the hallway, she encountered Paul, who was headed to his room to get his toiletry bag and something to sleep in.

"So you have attitude with me because your mother drank what she shouldn't have?" Paul said.

"Your mother had to take it to another level," Ginger said.

"My mother?" he responded. "I might have not had a good flight here, but I did notice that *your* mother had liquor in a flask on the plane. So who's zooming who?"

Ginger stormed off to the other room to get her mom's belongings. She thought Brenda was asleep, but she was not.

"Ginger, I'm so sorry," she said. "Sit down for a minute."

Ginger obliged her. "We didn't mean to ruin our Thanksgiving dinner. We took that first shot because your mother and I came to a truce and we drank to it. It was my idea."

"What was the truce?" Ginger asked.

"To make sure you and my son stay together," she answered. "We might be old—or older—but we're not blind or crazy. We knew you all have been having troubles for many months now. She blamed Paul; I blamed you.

"What we realized in spending some time together today is that sometimes it's nobody's fault. Sometimes things happen just through living. It's up to you and him to work it out. But we, as mothers-in-law, could help by being friends and not enemies.

"So, your mom asked for the second shot—for family. And that's why we got sick. Two shots. I haven't had a shot in forty years. It was too much."

"You all are something else," Ginger said. "I guess the best thing about it is that you all are now getting along after almost twenty years."

"In my heart, I only agreed to come on this trip to really learn about your mom, who she was, what she really was like. We never really spent any *real* amount of time together. Don't get me wrong: I wanted to come to Napa Valley. But that was another big part of my reason for agreeing to come."

"Wow," Ginger said, "the truth really is in the wine. And the tequila, too, I guess."

While that was going on, Madeline surprised Paul. "Don't go yet," she said as he was heading toward the door with his luggage.

"Huh?" Paul said.

"Can you sit down, for a minute?" Madeline said in a voice so low Paul had to strain to hear her. "The room is spinning but I want to apologize for that mess we caused down there tonight. I'm glad it didn't happen in the restaurant. I also wanted to say that I am glad you planned this trip.

"You probably didn't want me to come; I haven't been the best mother-in-law to you. Not because I don't like you or even love you—I do. It's just that Ginger has been my whole life. Do you know that when she was born, we both almost died? Yes, complications came up—I had some rare condition and my blood pressure dropped and it was all messed up—and they had to take her to save her. And her heart rate dropped, the cord was wrapped around her neck and she was breech.

"But she…we both made it. Doctors said we were little miracles. Your child will always be special to you, but she was even more special to me. So I am a little overboard when it comes to protecting her and wanting the best for her, no matter how old she is.

"But here's the thing: You are the best man for her—always have been."

And suddenly she was asleep. So, Paul gathered his things and headed to his mom's room. In the hallway, he and his wife's paths crossed again. The brief chat with their in-laws tempered their anger.

"Wild night, huh?" Paul said, smiling.

"Crazy," Ginger said. "I feel so bad for them. They are messed up. And we're supposed to have breakfast at nine and then start touring wineries."

"If they aren't up to it, we can drive around and see the area, eat and do wines later in the day—or the next day," Paul said. "We'll play it by ear."

"OK," Ginger said. "Let me go in here and check on this woman."

"I'll bring you a glass of wine later," Paul said. "Keep your phone near by. I'll text you."

But Paul never texted and it did not matter to Ginger; both listened to their respective mothers share news about themselves they never knew and were so shell-shocked by the information that they did not dare stop them. They listened…and listened…and listened until they fell asleep.

CHAPTER 10
HUNG-OVER & OUT

The morning brought less pain for Brenda and Madeline, but they were hardly themselves. Madeline went back to her room. She and Brenda showered and got dressed around ten o'clock and sat on the bed waiting for Ginger and Paul.

"I feel like a truck ran over me; then backed up and did it again," Brenda said.

"Same truck must have hit me, too," Madeline said. "My head doesn't hurt, but my stomach is not quite right and my body feels worn down."

"This is crazy," Brenda said, as Paul knocked on the door. "We're in the best area of the United States for wine and I don't want to even *see* a bottle of wine."

She opened it and Paul stood in the threshold, smiling, with two cups of coffee in his hands.

"OK, party animals," he said. "Here's a pick-me-up."

"Very funny," Brenda said, as she reached for a cup. "But this is exactly what I need."

"I don't even drink coffee, but if it's going to get me to feeling better, then I'll try some," Madeline said. "Where's Ginger?"

"She's gone down to get us a table for breakfast," Paul said.

He walked with the ladies to the elevator. "That was some night," he said. "I was feeling great about everything and then—"

"Do you really have to remind us, son?" Brenda asked. "It was embarrassing enough. Let's not relive it."

"I can't promise it won't come up again," Paul said.

"Did you get some pleasure out of us being so sick?" Madeline said.

"Pleasure? Seeing you all throw up in the hallway? Seeing you intoxicated?" Paul said. "Of course, not? But I did speak to both of you last night while you were in bed. Do you recall that?"

"You talked to me?" Madeline asked.

"No," Paul said, holding the elevator door open for them, "you talked to me."

"Oh my goodness," she said. "I don't remember that. What did I say?"

"That you love me and I'm the best thing that ever happened to Ginger," Paul said. "That's the abbreviated version."

And then he laughed, making Madeline uncertain if he was joking or telling the truth. The elevator doors opened and Ginger was standing right there.

"Oh, I was coming up to see where you all were," she said. "Hi, Mother. How you feeling? How are you, Ms. Wall?"

"OK," they said almost in unison.

"Well, the coffee should help," Ginger said. "And maybe some oatmeal and toast."

"That's about all I can take right now," Madeline said. They made their way to the restaurant.

"I hope no one remembers us from last night," Madeline said. "That was so embarrassing."

"I know," Brenda said. "I almost want to change hotels."

"Well, we're not doing that, Ma," Paul said. "We don't know them and they don't know us. So it really doesn't matter."

"You weren't the one who vomited in the lobby," Brenda said.

"Touché," he responded.

They made their way to their seats for breakfast. Paul and Ginger felt refreshed. They slept about seven hours.

"On the east coast, it's about one in the afternoon," Ginger said. "I'm hungry."

"My stomach doesn't feel quite right, but I'm eating because it's time to eat," Brenda said.

And so, everyone ate. Paul sat across from his wife and between his mother and mother-in-law. He felt a distance from Ginger that he could not pinpoint. He thought they had gotten past blaming each other's mother for their intoxication the night before, but knowing her, he sensed something was amiss.

"Gin, how you doing? How's your food?" he asked.

"Fine," she said without looking up. He knew then something was bothering her.

"What's wrong?" he asked. He figured she still blamed

his mother for her mom getting sick and throwing up.

"Nothing," she said.

The parents looked on, curiously.

"Come on, I know you," he said. "You can tell me. We're among family."

Ginger raised her head and looked at him. "Is there something you want to tell me?" she asked.

"Huh? No," he said. "Tell you about what?"

"About how you ended up out of work last year, which started all the drama we have had," she said.

Paul's heartbeat increased, but he remained outwardly calm—and did not say a word.

"Let's talk about it since you want to talk so much, since you want to know what's wrong with me," Ginger said.

"Maybe you should talk in private," her mother said.

"No, Paul said we're among family and I should say what's on my mind," Ginger responded. "So I'll ask again: Why did you lose your job?"

"What are you talking about?" Paul asked.

"I spoke to your mother last night," Ginger said.

"What?" Brenda said, shocked. "What are you talking about?"

"See, that's what a good buzz will do; you start telling stuff you didn't mean to tell," Ginger said. "You told me some harmless stuff and you also said, 'I know you have been having issues because of why Paul got *fired*."

"I did not say that," Brenda said with indignation.

"Ms. Wall, that's exactly what you said."

"Well, I don't remember that," Brenda added.

"Doesn't really matter if you remember," Ginger said. "It only matters if it's the truth. Paul, you told me you got downsized out of your job. But you told your mother something different. Why?"

"My mother is right," he said. "We should speak on this in private."

"No," Ginger said sternly. "Right now. What happened? You were fired? Why were you fired, Paul? I know why. I'm seeing if you're going to tell me the truth."

"It was some B.S.," he said.

"So it's true? You got fired and told me you got laid off," Ginger said. She was remarkably calm for someone so furious. "Why would you do that?"

"Because I was embarrassed," Paul said. "Embarrassed by what they did to me."

"No, if your mother is correct—," Ginger said.

"Ginger, I do not recall saying anything like this to you," Brenda said. "Where are you getting this from?"

"I got it from you, Miss Wall," Ginger said. "You said some nice things about me and about the marriage and then you told me your son got fired from his job because of sexual harassment."

"I knew that, but I wouldn't tell you," Brenda said.

"Why wouldn't you tell Ginger?" Madeline jumped in.

"Because it wasn't my place to," Brenda said.

Voices started to rise. "Wait, can we hold it down some?"

Paul said. "We already were embarrassed here last night."

Ginger ignored Paul.

"Well, you apparently felt like it was your place to go last night because you sure enough told me that," she said. "So the question is, Paul: Why didn't you tell me? You told your mother, but not your wife?"

"Gin, I didn't know what to do," Paul started.

"So it's true?" his mother-in-law asked with disdain in her voice.

"Gin, can we go somewhere for ten minutes to talk about this?" he asked.

"First of all, I'm not going anywhere," she said. "And secondly ten minutes hardly would be enough time for what I have to say to you."

Paul was trapped. There was no wiggle room, not an inch to squirm free. So he released the burden that he had been carrying around for nearly a year.

"It's true, but I didn't harass anyone," Paul said. "I'm sorry I lied to you, Gin. I really am. I didn't want you to think crazy about me because it's such a stupid reason to get fired."

"What did you do?" she asked, calmly. "It must have been really serious for them to let you go after—what?— fourteen years?"

"There was a woman on the job," he started. The eyes of the women were locked on him. The fall morning turned summer hot for Paul. "Her name was Sophia. She worked in the office. Any paperwork that I had to file after a job I had to file with her. So, one day she asks if I would like to go to the grand opening of an art gallery. I told her I would check with you and that I didn't know.

"I asked for her number to text her my answer. When I texted her that we already had plans, she started texting me all kinds of stuff. It was crazy, like she was cultivating a relationship in her head."

"What did she look like, Paul?" Madeline wanted to know.

"Ginger, can we finish this in private?" Paul asked.

"No, keep going," Ginger answered.

Paul took a deep breath. "She's an attractive woman, Ms. Knight. But that has nothing to do with anything."

The women did not respond.

"Before she switched up on me, we would exchange text messages about harmless stuff," he went on. "After about two weeks, we became really familiar with each other. She told me she was dating and so I didn't feel like there was anything there to be concerned with.

"Well, one day, Big Al sends me a text message. It's a short video of two people doing this sex trick where a guy flips the girl over and when they stop, they are in this wild sex position. Well, I forwarded it to her, to Sophia, and she took offense."

"You did *what*?" Ginger said. "You sent a video of two people having sex to a woman? Why would you do that? That's what you wanted to do to her? You didn't send it to me, but you sent it to some woman on your job?"

"You didn't want him to send that to you anyway, baby," Madeline said.

"Mother, please," Ginger said. "Paul, why would you send something like that to a woman?"

"It was a mistake," Paul said. "A grave mistake. I thought we were friends, like one of the guys. I shouldn't have done it, of course, looking back on it."

"So what's the B.S. part, Paul?" Ginger said. "You sent a woman a very inappropriate video. Doesn't seem like B.S. to me."

"It's B.S. because she then started going back through my text messages to her and started changing the meaning, changing the context of what I was saying. So, instead of my text reading: "Wanna meet at the Ritz for a drink?" she said it read like I was asking her out on a date or to spend the night at a hotel.

"She responded: 'Aren't you married?' It wasn't intended like she was insulted or anything like that. She meant it at the time like, 'Aren't you married? You've go to go home and be a husband.' That's one of the running jokes we had.

"She would ask me about doing something and I would tell her, 'No can do; going home to the wife.' And so it became this running joke with us where she would say, 'Aren't you married?' to almost anything I said."

"Now I see where the B.S. comes in—with you," Ginger said.

"Gin, that's not true," Paul pleaded. "Listen to the rest

of it. So, when she gets the video, all of a sudden our jokes became me harassing her. And because the video was pornography, they called it sexual harassment."

Ginger stared at him with so much anger. Paul did not know what to do, so he kept talking, thinking the longer she listened the clearer it would become to her. Wrong.

"It was crazy," he continued. "Here I thought she was a friend, but she turned out to be someone out to get me."

"Why was she out to get you?" Madeline asked.

"Because I would not go out with her," Paul said.

"You never met her out?" Ginger asked.

"No," Paul said. "I mean, she met all of us out a few times. It was never just her and me. She did talk about me rejecting her. She'd say, 'Married man, you need to loosen up a little. Every time I ask you something you say, 'I'm married.' So I think she simply was not used to a man being disciplined with her. And she didn't like it. I don't know what her motivation was because I never talked to her again. But she saved all our texts and inter-preted them to the mediator. Meanwhile, I didn't have any text messages because I deleted them all."

"Paul, this sounds crazy to me," Ginger said. "If there was nothing going on, if you didn't have an interest in this woman, why wouldn't you tell me about her? You never mentioned her name. I always asked who was with you when you would hang out. Never, not once did you mention a woman's name.

"So, because of that, it's hard for me to believe that

simple story. You lost your job because you were chasing another woman. Period."

"No, it's not as simple as that," Paul said. "I am not going to allow you to believe this nonsense."

"Nothing you can do to change it now," Ginger said. "I've been in the dark for eleven months. I came out here in good faith to mend our marriage. And yet I found out that you're a cheater and that you don't trust me enough to tell me something very personal, something that really affected our marriage, but you told your mother.

"Thanks for trusting in me."

And with that, Ginger tossed her cloth napkin onto the table and headed out of the hotel's front door. Madeline stood and stared at Paul before following her daughter.

"Ma," he said, looking at Brenda.

"Paul, I am so sorry," she said. "I promise you, I do not remember telling her you got fired. But I was so messed up that I guess I did. Maybe it was on my conscience and I didn't realize it."

"It's okay," he said. "It's my fault. I always hated not being upfront with her. Should have told her back then and faced the music."

"Well, you're going to have to talk to her—but when she cools off," Brenda said. "Saying something now is only going to make it worse. Trust me, I'm a woman."

"How can we go and have a nice day with her mad at me?"

"Easy," Brenda said. "She doesn't want to have a bad

time. Plus you have your momma here. Come on, let's go. They're probably outside waiting on us."

And they were. Paul used the remote to open the doors and physically opened the front passenger door for Ginger, who stepped into the car without acknowledging her husband.

Paul revealed a printout that had various wineries listed. "So, we can go to Beringer now and hit one or two others before the day is out. And we can stop somewhere for a nice lunch," he said. "Anyone have any thoughts on that?"

Ginger looked away from him, out the window. Madeline said, "I don't feel so great, so I'm not really ready to taste wines."

"Actually, me, either," Brenda said.

Paul was devastated. He was called "Vino" by his mother because he loved wine. He traveled to California on a plane despite his immense fear of flying. He was finally in his dream location with the closest women in his life...and no one wanted to go taste wine.

But he did not reveal his frustration. Not totally. "I can't believe I cannot get to a winery now that I'm finally in Napa," he said. "But we're a group traveling together, so it's not only about me."

He started the car and sat there for a moment or so.

"I have an idea," he said. "How about us taking a drive back toward San Francisco so we can see the Golden Gate Bridge during the day? We went across it, but it was too dark to really enjoy it. There's a park right there,

Golden Gate Park. We can go there and take some photos and take in the beautiful scenery.

"By the time we get back, it will be time for lunch and hopefully everyone will feel better and we can visit a winery. What do you think?"

"You know, you can walk across the Golden Gate," Madeline said. "Let's do that."

"That sounds like fun," Brenda said.

"I'm gonna leave that to you all," Paul said. "I'm sure it will be exciting, but flying here was exciting enough for me."

Ginger did not say anything. Paul hated when she was that way. He hated it because he did not know where her mind would go, but he knew it would not be a pleasant place.

"Gin, does this plan work for you?" he said.

"Fine," she said, not bothering to look in his direction.

"OK, well, I'm going to take the scenic route through downtown Napa so we can get a feel for where we are," he said.

Brenda pulled out her camera. Madeline fumbled with her phone. Paul lost himself in the moment as they rode through the charming and quaint town, laced with interesting shops and restaurants, with people milling about. The temperature was in the low sixties with the sun spraying rays over the place as if a spotlight.

"Magnificent time to be here," he said. "We could not have picked a better weekend."

"It is beautiful," Madeline said, but more to Brenda than Paul.

The foliage and yellow and red leaves in the trees and on the ground made for an image that one would see in a painting.

"I could live here," Paul said. "It's been ten minutes and I already know I could live here. It's so warm and so quaint. And it helps that there is wine all around you. I can be consumed in wine. OMG."

"It's interesting that you can love wine so much but not become a wino," Ginger's mother said.

"It's just like you liking alcohol but not becoming an alcoholic," Brenda said. She said it pleasantly, but she was defending her son, whether he wanted or needed it or not.

"I don't know if I like what you're insinuating," Madeline said.

"Don't get your Depends in a bunch," Brenda said, and everyone laughed, even Ginger.

"I'm glad to see some smiling faces in this car," Brenda added. "I'm feeling better and we should have a good time and enjoy each other."

"I agree with you, Ma," Paul said. Then he added: "OK, in honor of you ladies getting, uh, inebriated last night, why don't we share a story about an embarrassing moment that we haven't shared with anyone before."

"That's easy," Ginger said. "I married you."

"Ouch," Paul said. "That was mean. But at least you smiled. I like seeing you smile, Gin."

They were at a light before jumping on the highway headed toward the Golden Gate Bridge. They looked into each other's eyes for a few seconds before she looked away.

"Who wants to go first?" Ginger asked.

"I'm not sure what kind of story you're looking for, so Paul probably should go first," his mother said.

"OK," Paul said. "I'll go. Now, this has to be a story you never told anyone. OK? OK, about ten years ago, Helena had a school project where she had to take a coffee can, punch holes in the bottom of it and use it as a plant holder or something. I remember buying her one and then another one because something was wrong with the first one.

"So, this was a time you might remember, Gin. We were meeting in Buckhead at Phipps Plaza to go to the movies. It was the spring or fall—I can't remember which—but I had a pullover sweater on. So, anyway, I had a job in College Park and you were already in Buckhead, shopping or something. You had Helena with you. So, we were going to the movies and I rushed home, showered, changed clothes and got into the car to meet you all.

"Well, I am so anal about seeing the previews that I decided I would pass on going to the bathroom and would go when I got to the movies. So, I get on 85 North at the Connector and—bam—it's a logjam. Traffic is backed up for a few miles. So I'm anxious about getting to you all on time and I hate traffic and now I've got to go to the bathroom so bad that I'm squirming in my seat."

The ladies are laughing and hanging on to his every word. He went on: "So, we're at a standstill and I'm in the center lane with no way to take an exit. By the minute, I've got to go to the bathroom more and more. So I start looking around the car for a cup or bottle or anything because I'm about to pee on myself."

"Oh, my God," Madeline said.

"My mind is racing. Then it hits me: I bought that second coffee can and Helena left it in the trunk. So since we're at a standstill, I pop the trunk, get out of the car right there on 85 and hurry up and grab the coffee can and jump back into the car. I had no other option; I couldn't hold it much longer.

"So I'm frantically trying to open my pants, get the belt loose and the zipper down because I'm about to wet myself, which I could not let happen. I'm sweating. It's an emergency. I don't know how it is for women, but when a man has to pee badly and knows he's about to let it go, it's harder to hold it back.

"Finally, I get myself free and I position the can between my legs and—I'm sure you know the relief you feel when you've got to go really badly."

Paul started demonstrating behind the wheel his actions. He feigned closing his eyes and throwing his head back in relief. "I had saved myself and the relief felt so good," he said.

"But then I started feeling something. My butt got

warm. I looked down, and the can I was peeing in had holes in it. It was the first can I bought, not the second one. So all that pee that went in the can came right out in my seat."

The women howled, they laughed so hard. Paul was laughing hysterically, too, Then he started reenacting the moment. He pulled himself from his seat, as he did that night.

"I lifted my butt up so I wasn't sitting in a pile of pee," he said, and they burst into laughter again for several seconds. "It was a total mess. And once you start peeing, you can't stop."

Madeline and Brenda were falling all over themselves. Ginger was in tears. Paul, too. And he kept them in stitches.

"So I emptied my bladder and was sitting there on the highway in my own pee."

"Stop, Paul," his mother managed to get out between laughs. "You're crazy. I can't take any more. Please stop. Oh, my God."

But he wasn't finished. "So I was relieved in one sense, but soaking wet and pissy in another," he said, and Ginger buried her face in her hands, laughing so hard she could barely catch her breath.

"Paul, I don't believe you," she said.

"I'm serious," he said. "So now I have another problem. And we're still sitting in the same place; traffic had not moved. So I've got to do something. So I pop the trunk again to get some towels I have to wash the car out of the trunk to soak up some of all the pee on my seat."

The ladies again are doubled-over in laughter.

"I hurry up out of the car, hoping no one can see the big piss stain that covered my whole behind. I get the towels and place them on the seat and jump back into the car. I had about four towels, so they sopped up the urine pretty good."

He stopped to join the others in laughter. When he composed himself, he said, "So, I solve that crisis. I have gotten the pee off my seat. But my pants are soaking wet. Traffic starts to move a little bit and I almost swerved into someone because I was taking off my pants as I was driving."

Once again, there was laughter among the women. "You're killing me with this one," Brenda said.

"So, I use my feet to slip off my shoes and squirm my way out of my pants and drawers. I'm literally riding up 85 with my naked butt on a pile of pissy towels."

The women roll down the windows; they laughed so hard they got hot.

"So," Paul continued, "I've got about fifteen minutes max to get my underwear and pants dry."

"Oh, Lord," Ginger screamed.

"So, I turn the heat on blast and hold my drawers up to the vent."

"Ha, ha, ha, ha, ha, ha," the ladies howled.

"After about five minutes, they get mostly dry, but I'm sweating like a pig because it's burning up in there. Finally, we clear the congestion point and traffic starts to really flow. My drawers aren't quite dry, so I somehow get them to suspend on the vent so I didn't have to hold them up there. I roll down the window when I get past downtown and now I'm driving at about sixty-five miles an hour.

"So, I grab my pants and hang them out the window so they can dry as my drawers are drying."

Again, an eruption of laughter from everyone.

"I can't even imagine what that looked like: a half-naked man driving on the highway with his underwear stuck in a vent and his pants hanging out the window. The heat in the car worked good because my underwear got dry pretty quickly. They weren't fresh, but they were dry.

"I pull my pants from outside the window and position them so the wet area could take on the heat much of the way up 85 and all the way up Highway 400 to Lenox Road. By the time I get off at Lenox, the pants are not totally dry, but close to it. I put them up to my nose and was like, 'That's not good.' So, I park in the mall—you had called me twice but I couldn't pick up the phone with all that was going on.

"While sitting in the car I somehow got my stinky drawers on and pulled my stinky pants over top of them. And the only way I could think of to try to muffle the odor was to take off my sweater and wrap it around my waist."

"Oh, no," Ginger said. "I remember that night. You came in there looking crazy. And I asked you why you had your sweater around your waist. I remember."

"Well, I couldn't say, 'Because I pissed on myself and

I don't want you or Helena to smell it.' I don't know what excuse I gave you and I knew I looked crazy, but I had no alternative. It was a Harry Potter movie, maybe the first one, and Helena was so excited about it. I had to be there.

"You had already purchased the tickets and I went straight to the bathroom to wash my hands. I remember Helena wondering why I didn't hug and kiss her when I first saw you all, as usual. I made sure she sat between us because she would be so into the movie she wouldn't think about any odors. When the movie was over, you suggested we go somewhere for dessert. I was like, 'You and Helena go. I'll meet you at home.'

"And that's my embarrassing story that I had never told anyone."

The women shook their heads. "I don't think anything can top that," Madeline said. "I give you credit: I might not have *ever* told anyone that story. But it was hilarious. Oh, my God."

"And the way you told it," Ginger said. "I didn't realize you had that kind of comedic timing. Just hilarious."

"It's like you've been waiting to tell that story," Brenda said. "And it didn't take a buzz from wine to get it out of you."

"You know what else I remember about that night," Ginger said. "I found it curious then, but didn't say anything."

"What was that?" Paul asked.

"When Helena and I got home, you were taking a bath," she said, and they all burst into laughter again.

"Yes, I was," Paul said. "I needed a bath that night."

They all laughed some more before catching their breath.

"I will never look at you the same, son-in-law," Madeline said. "And I mean that as a compliment. You have way more of a sense of humor than I ever thought."

"I'm a funny guy," he said. "Well, maybe not funny, but I appreciate a good laugh as much as the next guy."

"That has to be one of the funniest stories I ever heard," Brenda said.

"I'll drink to that, literally," Paul said. "Ma, look in that bag between you two."

There she found two bottles of The Prisoner wine, a delicious California Zinfandel that traveled in his luggage, and four glasses. "I thought maybe we could have a little something to sip on while we drive," Paul said. "How are you all feeling?"

"Maybe that's what I needed—a good laugh—to feel better because I sure do," Madeline said.

"I can at least sip on a little," Brenda said.

"Here, let me open it," Ginger said.

"Paul, you're driving, so..." Ginger said.

"I know. I'll get some when we get to the park," he said. "But don't think I forgot: Somebody has to tell an embarrassing story."

"If we finish these two bottles of wine, I'll be glad to tell a couple of stories," Madeline said.

"OK, I'll tell one now," Ginger said. "It won't be as long as Paul's but I never told this to anyone."

"Oh, really," Paul said. "OK, I'm ready for this."

"All right, so I get a promotion on my job to senior marketing analyst," Ginger began, "and the men in the office are livid. You know how men are—well, you might not, Paul, but I'm sure our parents do. They think women are inferior and should advance only so much.

"Well, I earned the promotion and my boss was courageous enough to give it to me knowing how the men in the office would react. So, anyway, I have a week to make this big presentation in front of my boss, his boss and the men who were angry I got the job.

"I prepared my butt off to make this presentation awesome. I needed to impress everyone. So, I go to the salon and get my hair done. I bought a beautiful new suit. I'm ready.

"I start my day as I usually do: with a light breakfast of juice and yogurt and a cup of coffee. I'm totally prepared. We get into a boardroom and I'm looking great and feeling great. I'm about to nail it, and make those guys look silly.

"So I get introduced and I get up to the head of the table where I have my stuff set up on an easel. I start great, talking about our competitor's approach to this particular project, and I can see in my boss' face how proud he is that he promoted me. But then it happened: I turned to point out something on the easel and as soon as I turned my back totally to them, I let out the loudest fart you could imagine."

Paul, Madeline and Brenda screamed in laughter. "Are you serious?" Brenda asked.

"Totally," she said.

"Wow," Madeline said. "You never told me that."

"What did you do?" Paul said.

"Well, first of all, it wasn't merely loud, but it was stinky," Ginger said, and the laughing began again.

"So I'm standing up there, afraid to even turn around to see their faces. But when I do turn around, it's like the funk rushed up my nose. And it was so strong that it jolted me; I couldn't hide on my face that it stunk to high hell."

More laughter.

"So I'm standing there, gagging on my own fart, and they are looking at me and trying to pretend they didn't hear it or smell it."

More laughter.

"So what did you do?" Paul said, finally.

"I looked at them with a straight face and said, 'That's what I think of the competition.'"

Paul, Brenda and Madeline laughed loudly, just as the men in the boardroom had.

"I can't even tell you how embarrassed I was," Ginger said. "The funny thing is that after that, I was even more loose and the guys even loosened up and somehow, my fart at the wrong time helped me and those guys have a better relationship. Don't get me wrong; I don't trust them. But from that moment on they stopped being so rude and distant with me. So it's made for a better working environment."

"Wow," Brenda said. "It takes passing gas to get men to respect you. How crazy is that?"

They settled down and the attention turned to wine.

"This is some good wine, Vino," Brenda added. "I'm feeling much better."

"Look at that," Paul said, pointing to the Golden Gate Bridge.

"Beautiful," Madeline said.

Paul drove across the bridge, slowly, and the magnificence of the view quieted the car. No one said a word. They snapped photos and admired the prodigious bridge and skyline of San Francisco off in the distance.

"Just beautiful," Ginger said.

Paul took the first exit over the bridge and worked his way back and crossed the bridge again, headed toward Napa. Dozens and dozens of people walked across the bridge.

"Look, Brenda," Madeline said. "That's gonna be us."

"But, Paul," Brenda said, "we're not walking back across, so you're going to have to come pick us up on the other side."

The traffic was heavy going back across the bridge, which was fine to the ladies; they got to take more photos and enjoy the cloudless day even more. Once they parked at Golden Gate Park, they stood outside the car and enjoyed the wine.

"I'm gonna need to walk off this wine," Brenda said. "I'm feeling it."

"Let's do it," Madeline said. "You walking with us, Ginger?"

"I think I'm going to pass," she answered. "I want to admire this view, enjoy this wine and relax. That's what a vacation is to me."

So off the seniors went, leaving Paul and Ginger in the park. She did not wait long to address her concerns. All that laughing in the car made her feel good, but it did not eliminate the angst she had about how Paul lost his job and that he did not tell her.

"I don't understand; how am I supposed to feel?" Ginger said. "You told me you got laid off, but you got fired. And you got fired because of sexual harassment. How can I believe anything you say?"

"Oh, so it's the 'Boy Who Cried Wolf' thing, huh?" Paul said. "Nothing I say is the truth? I've lied so much that you can't believe anything that comes out of my mouth? Well, if you truly believe that, then what I have to say about it won't matter. If you don't believe that— which I hope you don't—then maybe we can get past this.

"Gin, it is very simple: I sent the woman an inappropriate text message with the video. That was it. I told her repeatedly that I'm a married man. I have tried to figure out why she would turn on me like she did and I'm guessing it was because I never bit on her advances. They were subtle, but they were also obvious. And I stuck to: 'I'm going home to the wife.'"

"Do you understand that even if what you said is true," Ginger said, "the violation and the dishonoring of our marriage is in you having these private jokes and text messages; you were building a relationship with her. And if she didn't get offended by the video, you'd still have this secret relationship with her. That's the violation and the disrespect.

"If you felt compelled to never mention her to me— not even say her name—then it shows there was something to hide, or something you thought you'd want to hide in the future. And that's hard to swallow.

"I can think you asked me for a divorce because you were going to run away with whatever her name is. I could believe that you decided to try to stay in the marriage because she broke up with you. I could believe that you could still have something going with her. I could start thinking about those times you said you worked late—were you really working or working with Sophia?

"You see what I'm saying? This kind of thing triggers a whole lot of distrust and a whole lot of questions—and none of it is good."

Ginger's points were so valid that Paul pondered them for a minute or so. He looked off in the direction of the bay, with Alcatraz in the far-off distance. He did not want to react to what she said right away. To do that could mean he was more interested in reacting than actually listening, and he did not want her to think that. So he didn't say anything. And he didn't know what to say.

Finally, Ginger leaned on the car hood beside him.

"I'm sorry," he said. "I get it. The things I thought were harmless clearly they aren't harmless, even if I had no intention of doing anything with her. I'm really sorry, Gin."

"I'm not going to play holier-than-thou with you," she said. "You know, laughing in the car about your peeing on yourself was such a good thing for me. It helped me purge some of the really bad feelings I had about you. They didn't all go away. I'm not saying that.

"But what I'm saying is that even when I was laughing, I was thinking: 'He's a good man and we've had a good life together.' The last year or so has been hell. But here we are, in California. It could be worse."

Paul put his arm around his wife and looked at her. She did not look at him; she looked straight ahead.

"Gin," he said softly, "I'm sorry. Nothing like that will ever happen again. I promise. I love you."

She slowly nodded her head. With his arm still around her shoulder, he lowered it and rubbed her back. It was another of the delicate affections he used to show her early in their marriage.

And Ginger began to cry—at first tears sliding down her face and then downright weeping. Paul hugged her tightly, with both arms. He was alarmed. He knew his wife, and the way she cried was a sorrowful cry, not tears she might shed in a time of personal turmoil.

"What's wrong?" he asked.

"Nothing," she said.

"You're crying; something must be wrong," Paul said.

"We've been through a lot," Ginger said. "As soon as we take one step forward, there's one step back. I'm worn out."

"Stay here," Paul said. "We need to finish this bottle—and open the other one, too."

He went into the car and poured the last of the wine in their glasses. Ginger wiped her eyes and took a deep breath as Paul stood in front of her with the wine.

"I will do anything to get us past this," Paul said. "Let's take in the moment. Look at where we are. It's a beautiful day. Look at that bridge above us and the mountains and the city over there and the boats…and you cannot get much more picturesque than this. We have to enjoy it. We have great wine and a perfect day. No more crying, no more negative anything. Let's live."

"You said you'd do anything for us to get past this," Ginger reminded him.

"I don't like the way you said that," Paul noted. "But I *did* say it. Why?"

"I want to walk across the Golden Gate Bridge," she said.

"Gin," Paul said, "not that. We're sitting here enjoying the amazing view, sipping on wine. It's lovely."

"How we gonna let our mothers do it, but not us?"

Ginger said. "That's crazy. Imagine what the view is from up there. And we can put our wine in a cup and—"

"A cup?" Paul said. "Wine is not to be consumed in a foam cup," Paul said.

"You know what you sound like? An English snob without the accent," Ginger cracked. "You can do it. You flew all the way across the country to get here… You said you'd do anything."

"Wine relaxes me," he said. "Let's finish this up and then I'll do it—only because I want to make things right with us."

CHAPTER 11
BRIDGING THE GAP

Paul finished his wine, and another glass, before they embarked on the journey across the Golden Gate Bridge. Oh, and he carried some in a foam coffee cup, too.

He decided he'd talk as much as possible to keep his mind off of what he was doing.

"Do you know the bridge is seventy-five years old?" he said as they made their first steps across it. "I read up on it. It was built in 1937. It took almost four years to build."

Ginger sensed what Paul was doing, so she engaged him. "Tell me more," she said as she looked out at the stunning view. Paul kept talking, but she was mesmerized by the beauty and hardly heard him.

"Ok," Paul said, "the bridge is one-point seven miles long. So, it should take us about an hour and a half to walk it. We'll probably catch up with our mothers at some point.

"During construction, eleven men died falling off this bridge. They had this safety net hanging below the bridge and when men fell, it would catch them. Those who fell in it were entered into the 'Halfway-To-Hell Club.' It caught nineteen men.

"But eleven men died when a part of the scaffolding collapsed and ripped through the net. That's crazy, right?"

Ginger didn't answer.

"Here's what's even more crazy," Paul added. "More people have committed suicide jumping off this bridge than anyplace else in the country. There was a documentary I saw called 'The Bridge' that actually showed some of the twenty-four suicides off this bridge in 2004 alone. Now that's crazy."

"Yeah, it is," Ginger said. "I hope no one does that today, while we're up here… Paul, look. Look out there."

There were a plethora of sailboats elegantly drifting in the water, decorating the bay with brilliant colors. A few clouds seemingly strategically placed gave the image the feel of a painting.

Paul looked, and the view was so breathtaking that he stopped talking.

"My God," he said. He sipped his wine. "Unbelievable. I imagined it would be beautiful, from what I saw while driving across the bridge. But this? This is crazy beautiful."

Ginger looked up at him. "I know," she said. "You cannot tell me there is not a God. Man built this bridge. But all that out there…the water, the island, the mountains, the sky…that's God's work."

They walked the next five minutes without saying a word. Ginger could hardly take her eyes off the view. Paul watched the people. He could tell the locals; they walked briskly and hardly glanced to admire the stunning scenery. The first-timers or visitors took it in slowly, walking at a deliberate pace while stopping often to take and pose for photos.

"Since I'm up here," Paul said, "we might as well get a picture."

"You're gonna need to get up against the rail," Ginger said.

"OK," Paul said with confidence that he did not have. But he decided to do it instead of thinking about it.

So, he stopped at an angle where Ginger could capture the magnificent San Francisco skyline behind him. But people walked by, between them, so she had to wait a few minutes before it was clear to take the photo.

In the interim, Paul sipped his wine and then made the mistake of looking straight down at the water. The combination of the waves, the height at which he stood and his fear of heights, set off a minor scare. It was like the blood in his body was draining.

But he was determined to not let it mess up his experience. So he closed his eyes for a few seconds and told himself, "Hold it together." When he opened them, he was a different person. He felt relaxed, like wine can induce, but also alert and excited.

He posed showing the "peace" sign and smiled the biggest smile he had in some time. He felt on top of the world, literally and emotionally.

Paul again looked down over the railing at the waves, to test himself. Bad move. He got dizzy and disoriented. Ginger could see it coming on and immediately came to his aid.

"Here," she said, putting his cup of wine to his mouth. "Concentrate on this."

It worked. Paul pulled himself together rather quickly and they continued their walk—hand-in-hand.

Ginger looked down when Paul clutched her hand to make sure what she felt was real.

"You have not held my hand in at least ten years, Paul," she said. "These changes in the last month or so have been dramatic. Maybe I should get you drunk so you'll finally tell me what's really going on because it has to be something."

Paul smiled. He looked up at the expanse of the bridge and the view beyond it to take in the beauty of it all. And it almost came out right then. He wanted badly to tell Ginger that they were millionaires and their lives, as they knew it, had changed.

Telling her right there, on the Golden Gate Bridge, would be symbolic of how he felt about their future— they were above the world. But his mom was not around, and in his mind, he wanted to tell all three of the women at the same time at the top of the mountain at the Sterling Vineyard. That was the new plan he came up with. So, he held back, hard as it was.

About a half-mile in front of them were Brenda and

Madeline, who were becoming faster friends. They walked at a much less brisk pace than their children. And they talked the entire time, learning that they had been compatible all along.

"Finally," Madeline said, looking down at her cell phone.

"What?" Brenda wanted to know.

"Mitch finally texted me back," she said.

"OK, what did he say?"

"He said he has a friend for you and that they will be here either tonight or tomorrow night. We can decide."

"I'd like them to come now, but it's probably better that they come tomorrow," Brenda said. "This is our first night. We probably shouldn't separate from the kids tonight."

"That's true, but if I know my daughter, she will try to escort us tomorrow," Madeline said. "It amazes me that she tries to be the mother sometimes. I agree tomorrow is the better day to do it, but…"

"But Paul will be all in it, too," Brenda said. "I guess it's better than them just saying, 'Do whatever.' We should talk to them about it tonight so they'll be clear about it tomorrow."

"Should I ask about his friend?" Madeline said. "We should know something about him before he gets here."

"Yes, you should call him," Brenda said.

And Madeline did. "I'm glad you called because it took me ten minutes to type that text message," Mitch said. "Texting for me is only in case of emergency, if I'm tied up in a truck and being kidnapped or something."

Madeline laughed. "You're funny."

They chatted and laughed and Brenda got a little jealous. She could see how much Madeline enjoyed Mitch and looked forward to seeing him, and Brenda did not have that in her life. She was not "hating" on her new friend, but she *was* envious.

"So what's up with his friend?" she asked.

Madeline said, "His name is Lionel and he's retired military, too. He says Lionel is a fun man, a good man."

"Yeah, but that doesn't mean his interesting," Brenda said. "But, at this point, how can I complain? Let's see what happens."

Madeline set it up for the men to drive to Napa from Sacramento and meet them for dinner the next night. "My son-in-law did a lot of research," she told Mitch." So I'm sure he will have some place to recommend for us."

"You know what?" Brenda asked. "This walk has been great for my energy and my stomach. I feel a lot better."

"Me, too," Madeline said. "Almost like new. By the time we get back to Napa Valley, I'll be ready to really eat."

Brenda's phone rang before she could respond. It was Paul.

"We're almost on the other side," Brenda said. "How's the park?"

"I don't know because we left the park," Paul said.

"What? Well, where are you?" she asked.

"Right behind you," he answered.

Brenda turned around to see her son and daughter-in-law about twenty yards behind them.

"Look," she said to Madeline.

"Oh, my goodness," Madeline said. "I thought you were going to stay at the park and pick us up on this side of the bridge."

"We couldn't let you all outdo us," Paul said.

Madeline looked down at their clutched hands and smiled. She had viewed Paul as a slouch—or at least someone who was a good man but not a great achiever, which is what she wanted for her daughter. So, while she never protested Ginger's choice for a husband, she never gave him a ringing endorsement or fully embraced him.

Watching Paul with Ginger on the trip gave her an appreciation for her son-in-law that she did not have. She listened to him speak, *really* listened, and determined that he was much smarter than she realized and much more cultured and definitely far more humorous. She, indeed, took him to be a humorless person, someone who could not enjoy a good joke and could not tell one.

His self-deprecating story on their way to the Golden Gate Bridge shed a new light on Paul, the man. Seeing him hold her daughter's hand gave Madeline a much more favorable feeling about him.

At the same time, Brenda assessed Ginger—and told her so.

"Can I steal your wife from you for a few minutes?" Brenda said, grabbing Ginger's free hand.

Paul didn't answer. He released her hand and they walked in front of Paul and Madeline.

"I want to tell you," Brenda began, "that already I have seen more of who you are since yesterday than I have in almost twenty years. And you know why that is? Because I probably wasn't looking before now. Why that was the case, I cannot really explain except to say that as a parent, you can sometimes see your child as so special that no one is really good enough for him.

"I have seen the kind of mother you are and I have seen how nice a house you keep and how hard you work. But I couldn't pull myself to believe you were right for Paul. And I'm sorry for that."

"But what has happened for you to feel differently, Ms. Wall?"

"My son is perfect to me but he's not perfect," Brenda said. "He has his little—what do they call them?—idio-syncrasies. And I see where you manage them very well. You got him to get on an airplane. Let's start with that. And even though you didn't sit with him—and even though I was drinking with your mother—I saw how you checked on him and reassured him, helped him get through it. I saw that you really cared—even though things haven't been that great with the marriage. I know what's going on—some of what's been going on. I com-mend you for that."

"Thanks, but I've always cared about Paul and always tried to be a good wife," Ginger said. "We've had our problems, but no more than anyone else. I would like to ask you something, though."

"Go ahead," Brenda said.

"In the last month or so, Paul has been different," Ginger said. "He's been happy and positive and it has thrown me off."

"I noticed the same thing," Brenda said. "I actually was gonna ask you if you knew what was going on with him."

"What are y'all talking about?" Paul said from behind them.

"You," they said in unison, and laughed.

"Forget it," Paul said. "I don't even wanna know."

"Well, I know this," Madeline said. "I'm not walking back across that bridge."

"I'll go back and get the car," Paul said. "I'll call you when I cross the bridge and turn around."

"Paul," Ginger said, "you sure you don't want me to go with you? I don't feel so good, but I'll go with you if you want me to."

He smiled. "You do care about me," he said. "If you're tired, you should stay with them. I'll be fine. I can walk a little faster so I can get back here as quickly as possible."

Paul went on his way, and the ladies crossed the bridge and found a place where they could rest and talk.

"Might as well tell you this now, Ginger," Madeline said. "We have a dinner date tomorrow night."

"Excuse me?" Ginger said. "A dinner date? With who?"

Madeline explained and Ginger was not happy.

"I don't think that's the point of us coming out here," she said. "You don't really know these men. And you think I'm going to let you run off with them? I don't think so."

"I wasn't asking your permission, child," Madeline said. "I am your mother, not the other way around. I was giving you the courtesy of letting you know what we were going to do. I know this man and it's not like we're in jeopardy—or that we won't be in a public place."

Ginger turned to Brenda. "Have you told Paul this?" she asked.

"Not yet," she answered. "And I'm sure he will have the same feelings as you, that we shouldn't go. But we're not some young kids who don't know what we're doing. We invented dating."

She and Madeline laughed. Ginger did not. And the look on her face told of her over-the-top concern. She had read about the Craigslist killer and the guy who met a woman on Christian Singles.com and killed her. Ginger could not see any good in them going out with men they hardly knew.

"Why is it that you young folks think we don't know what we're doing?" Brenda asked.

"Exactly," Madeline chimed in. "We raised you. I taught you how to deal with young boys and then men. So you know I know what I'm talking about because you've told me as much. So, it really comes down to this: You think I have lost it as I have gotten older? You think all the stuff I shared with you has somehow departed my mind and I'm some lost little girl going out into the dating world?"

"I'm not saying that, Mother," Ginger said. "I'm saying that things are different now. People are more crazy than ever and you have to be careful about who you sit across from at dinner."

The back-and-forth went on for several minutes, with neither side budging. Finally, Paul called to say he had crossed the bridge in the rental car and had turned around and was headed their way. He met them near the tollbooth and they jumped in the car and headed back toward Napa.

"By the time we get back, it'll be time for lunch," Paul said. "You all feeling better? Think you'll be ready to eat? I found this cool place online where we could stop and eat outside if it's warm enough when we get there."

No one said anything. "Hello?" Paul said. "OK, what happened?"

"These senior citizens are talking about they're going on a blind date tomorrow night," Ginger blurted out.

"Oh, now we're senior citizens?" Brenda said.

"You're not too old for me to whip your butt," Madeline said.

"Wait a minute," Paul said. "What do you mean?"

"What she means is that my friend, Mitch, is visiting his cousin in Sacramento and he and his friend, Lionel, are going to come up and take me and Brenda to dinner tomorrow night," Madeline said.

"You have a problem with that?" Brenda asked, almost daring her son to challenge her.

"Ah, yes, I do, as a matter of fact," Paul said. "Who are these people? And I thought this was a family trip."

"It is a family trip, and us having dinner with someone else will not take away from it, Paul," Brenda said. "And you and your wife can have a nice dinner together without us around. It works out for everyone."

"Why can't we all have dinner together?" Paul asked. "The six of us."

"Because we don't need you and Ginger trying to chaperone us," Brenda said. "What are we? Teenagers?"

"I can't believe we're still talking about this," Madeline said. "We appreciate your concern. But we're not going skydiving or mountain climbing. We're having dinner. So relax."

"And I don't want to talk about it anymore," Brenda said.

Paul drove on and glanced over at Ginger, who shook her head.

"Wait, what, exactly, is the problem?" Madeline said. "Could you please tell me? If it's something more than you thinking we shouldn't go with them because they are men and we don't know them that well, you can keep quiet. But if there is more to it, then please share with me."

Again, Paul's and Ginger's eyes met.

"Well," Ginger began, "it's basically like this: I've never seen you with another man or even heard of you with another man or even conceived of you with another man. It was always you and Daddy; that's all I know.

"So to tell me you're planning to go out with someone, well, that doesn't sit well with me. And I realize it might sound crazy; I do. I'm a fully grown woman but you're still my mother."

"I appreciate that, baby," Madeline said. "But your dad—God rest his soul; he was a good man who was good to me—but he's gone. It took me a while to accept it, to deal with it. I'm *still* dealing with it. But it has been almost a year and I have got to live my life, whatever time I have left. And it's not like I'm trying to marry this man. I met him at church and I have seen him a few times.

"He lives in San Diego, but he happens to be visiting his family near here. Why wouldn't we see each other? What's the harm? And above all, why wouldn't you trust me enough to enjoy the company of a man without dishonoring your father? And I knew him better than anyone in the world. Your dad would not want me mourning him for the rest of my life."

Ginger appreciated her mom's points.

"If he's her friend," Paul asked his mother, "how did you get involved in this, Ma?"

"Because I asked Maddy to ask if he had a friend," she answered. "Why not? I'm single. I like adult male attention, too. And don't bring up your father. I'm sure he's living his life, which is what he should do. I have to live mine."

Neither Paul nor Ginger had any retort of consequence, so they rode on in silence, admiring the wonderful landscape.

When they got into Napa, they took Route 29 all the way in to St. Helena, a quaint little mountainside town in the heart of the Valley. And they really liked it because of its name, Helena, same as their daughter. They admired the wineries they passed along the way: Beringer, Sutter Homes, Peju, Milat, and the endless row of restaurants and shops that begged for a visit.

"You feel like eating?" Brenda said to Madeline.

"I finally feel like myself, for the most part," she answered. "Well, at least I can eat. My body isn't quite right, but that walk did me good. Shoot, I'll be ready for some wine with lunch."

"I have a cool place for us to eat," Paul said. "It's up ahead, I think. Looked it up on the Internet. It's called Gott's Roadside."

"There it is," Brenda said, pointing to the left. And so it was. It had an American flag hanging in front, high above the street, and a huge patio filled with umbrellas, people everywhere and smoke rising from its chimney.

"It must be good because it's packed," Madeline said.

"Very cute," Brenda added.

Paul parked the car and they made their way in and ordered. They were lucky; they were able to secure a table under an umbrella up against the white picket fence that surrounded the patio.

Madeline had the Chinese Chicken Salad, Brenda the

Shrimp Tacos, Ginger a bowl of chili and a Classic Tuna Melt and Paul the Classic Tossed Cobb Salad and garlic fries. He also ordered a bottle of LaFollette 10 Pinot Noir for thirty-three-dollars.

"Can't have good food without good wine," Paul said. And no one argued with him.

Madeline said grace and they ate. "Hey," Paul said, looking at his and Ginger's moms, "you all think you're slick. You were supposed to tell us an embarrassing story that you haven't told anyone."

"That's right," Ginger said. "Who's going first?"

"I'm not sure I can tell you mine now; we're eating," Madeline said.

"That's a cop out," Brenda said.

"OK, fine," Madeline said. "You have to get closer because I don't want to say this too loudly."

Everyone leaned in. "It's not a long story," she began. "I was about twenty-two and dating this guy that I really liked. He was strong and smart and funny and he liked me for me."

"Sounds like Daddy," Ginger said.

"Ha, ha. It *was* your Daddy," Madeline said. "So, we're dating like three months and we'd never been intimate. We spent a lot of time together because we enjoyed each other so much. I was holding out—not because I wasn't attracted to him or even really liked him. I was in love with him and I had to make sure he respected me.

"You know how men can put you in a category if you're too forward. They start thinking you're that way all the time and never once consider that you could only be that way with them because of something they did with you that freed you up."

"Right," Brenda jumped in. "Don't get me started with the double standard of how women are viewed by men."

"That's a whole different talk show," Madeline said. "But anyway, I had to make sure that he knew I wasn't easy. So, I was having a hard time sleeping and took some sleeping pills one night right before he came over to my place. My mother was sick, I was thinking about graduate school; there was a lot on my mind and when it was time for bed, I would lie there on my back, looking at the ceiling.

"Well, I also had been sick—stomach problems—and when I was growing up there was no such thing as hot mint ginger tea. My mom gave us a laxative. So that's what I took to feel better."

"Uh-oh," Brenda said. "I see where this is going."

No one else did. "So, he's over my apartment," Madeline went on. "We're talking and having a good time and it's about two or three in the morning and we're both asleep on the couch. When I woke up, I couldn't ask him to go home.

"So I tell him to come on, 'Let's go to bed.' He perks right up and I guess thinks we're gonna do something. Anyway, I change into a gown and he's in bed in his boxers. And we're hugging and kissing and I'm so tired that as soon as we stop, I fall asleep. The sleeping pills took over.

"I guess after a while your dad fell asleep, too. Around six in the morning, I wake up. The pills were so strong that I'm a little bit disoriented. I see him resting there peacefully. The sun is peeping through the blinds. Just a perfect little morning.

"Then I start to smell something. I start sniffing him, seeing if it's coming from him. I sit up in the bed and I'm looking around the room, and the scent is getting stronger and stronger. Now it's plain old stinky. So I move the sheets back and the funk bursts into my face. Again, I thought he had passed gas. But the reality was crazy."

Madeline leaned in even closer so that she could lower her voice and they could still hear her. "It turned out that it wasn't him," she said. "I looked between my legs and there was a small pile of shit in the bed, all runny and wet. I had shit on myself in my sleep."

The group burst into laughter so loud that almost everyone on the patio turned to see what was happening. Paul got up from his seat and leaned over the white picket fence, laughing uncontrollably.

It took them a few minutes to get themselves together.

"Mother," Ginger said when it calmed down. "Are you serious?"

"The moral of this story?" Madeline asked. "Don't take a sleeping pill and a laxative at the same time."

And the laughter started again. It took them a few minutes to calm down.

"I tell you what," Brenda said. "If he married you anyway, he really loved you."

"Wait," Paul said, "how did you explain to him what happened?"

"Oh, well, that was funny, too," Madeline said. "So, I was, as you might guess, panicked when I realized what happened. So I tried to cover up the pile with the sheets to mute the funk and then ease out of the bed without waking him. But all the movement woke him up. So, I tried to hurry to the bathroom, but it was on his side of the bed, so I had to walk right past him.

"Remember that nightgown I said I put on? Well, it was white and the back of it looked like I sat in a giant pile of dark chocolate. It was crazy. I tried to hide it but there was too much mess."

Laughing, Ginger asked, "What did Daddy say?"

He said, "You OK?"

"I hope you said, 'No,'" Brenda said.

"I did. I told him to not move; I didn't want him to—God forbid—roll over onto that mess or pull the cover off of it. So, he just lay there. I cleaned myself up and told him to get out of the bed as I pulled the sheets off.

"He never said a word. He just looked at me. And I never said anything about it. It was so stinky and nasty. But that's the kind of man he was: He didn't want me to be any more embarrassed than I already was."

"No offense, but he still married you?" Paul said. "Now that's love."

"So if that were me, you wouldn't have asked me to marry you?" Ginger said.

"Gin, you can do-do right here and I'd clean it up and keep it moving," Paul said. Everyone laughed, and the tension over their mothers' double date the next day was gone.

"I have never told anyone that story; I actually tried to forget it," Madeline said.

"When you really think of it, it's romantic," Ginger said. "You showed yourself at a vulnerable position and Daddy still wanted you. It didn't matter to him. He did not care. He loved you."

Paul poured everyone more wine. "See, this is what I'm talking about," he said. "A beautiful day, good food, good wine, lots of laughs and family."

"How you feeling, Mother?" Ginger said. "Your stomach."

"I feel like I'm back to normal," Madeline said. "Bring on the wine tasting."

"I feel a little sluggish, but I'm ready to go, too," Brenda said.

"Speaking of going, it's your time to go," Paul said. "What's your embarrassing story?"

"I haven't had enough wine yet to tell it," she said. "Let's keep drinking and go to a tasting and then let me tell my story."

No one argued with Brenda. They had laughed so hard at Madeline that they needed a break anyway. So they enjoyed the mid-sixties November temperatures and absorbed being in Napa Valley.

"I said it already, but I could live out here," Paul said. "There's a feel of peace and calm out here that I never had before."

"Yes, but I'm sure it's the idea that there is wine all around you that makes it even more appealing," his mother said. "Look out there. Vineyards everywhere."

Ginger wanted to talk about something else. "I probably didn't handle it well on the bridge, but can I ask you something, Mother— and you, too, Miss Wall?" she asked.

The ladies nodded their heads.

"It hasn't even been a year ago since Daddy died and I haven't gotten over it," she began. "I still dream about him being here and I wake up so devastated and even angry when I realize that it was a dream. I can admit—I was a daddy's girl and I haven't moved on. I want my father here. So, how do you do it? How do you move on?"

Madeline took the defensive at first. She didn't want her daughter to think she loved her father any more than she loved him as her husband. But she surprised herself by her ability to eschew her personal feelings and, instead, seek to give Ginger some clarity.

Madeline sipped her wine and motioned for Paul to pour her more. He did and she took a sip of it and reached across the table and held her daughter's hand.

"I guess we're one big happy family here, so I can share this right here, right now," Madeline started. "I miss your father more than anyone could possibly know. You don't love him or miss him any more than me, I can promise you that. I can hardly remember my life before him. His love is infused in my body, in my heart. No one could ever replace who he was to me, who he remains to me, even in death. I learned how to love through your father. Everything good in me came from my parents and your dad.

"I am so glad to hear how much you love and miss him. It's only right because you were the crown jewel of his life. He loved me, sure. He coveted you, Ginger. You know what he said one time? He said, 'Maddy, I can die a proud man knowing I helped bring my daughter into the world.' That's how much you meant to him—everything.

"So I guess you thinking I must be crazy to not still be totally devastated by his death. But you're wrong, honey. Do you have any idea how upside down my life has been since he died? Do you have any inkling what it is like to have one of your arms cut off? That's what it is like for me.

"So, my answer is, I don't know how to tell you to move on. I'm living my life, but I haven't moved on. This man lives in me every day and always will. I knew him better than anyone on the planet. He shared so much with me, and me with him. And because I know him, I know he hardly wants me sitting around playing the victim and not living my life. That's the man he was.

"I never dishonored my husband in life and I damn sure won't in death. And he would want me to live my life. I have to, Ginger. If I don't, what happens to me? I don't have my husband anymore and you can rest assured I'm not OK about that. I have the same dreams you have about him being here, only to wake up in tears. We got sick last night and while I was in bed, I thought about how he would have reacted to me throwing up in the hallway of a hotel. And you know what? He would have made sure I was all right, cleaned up the mess and once I started feeling better, laughed his ass off at me. He would have made me laugh at myself.

"Think about it: He never ran stuff into the ground. He was always about moving on to the next thing. He was positive, Ginger. And so I'm not going to be the widow so devastated that she sits in the house with the shades drawn. And you know why? That's not what my husband would want me to do. And so I am honoring him by living my life. And that's what you have to tell yourself and believe it. Your father wants you to live your life."

With that, Madeline wiped the tears that streamed down her face. Ginger did, too. And so did Brenda. Paul practically popped an eye muscle he worked so hard to prevent crying.

In a very real way, one he never articulated, this was the kind of thing Paul wanted to happen on their trip. The more he thought of their parents going with him and Ginger, the more he thought it was an ideal way to bring the families together for more than holidays, graduations or funerals.

There was a divide between the families stemming from

unfounded perspectives. Brenda perceived Madeline's self-assuredness as arrogance and snobbishness and Madeline interpreted Brenda's unfiltered tongue as a lack of sophistication. Their discord was as transparent as glass, and so the families hardly spent time truly getting to know each other because Brenda and Madeline spread misleading rumors and sometimes all-out lies about their child's spouse's family.

It was pathetic, yes, but it was their way. Paul saw this cross-country venture as an opportunity to end the madness, to bring together the families and form a bond. It was a truly noble idea, especially with women in their sixties who were stuck in their ways, however warped.

But it was working. Something about being away from home opened them up, batted down their guards and they allowed the other to see her for who she really was. Madeline's explanation to Ginger silenced the table, except for the tears.

Paul looked at his mother and he knew she had a new respect, a new appreciation for Madeline.

"Let's have a toast to your husband," Paul said, as the women wiped away tears.

Ginger rose from the table and came over to the other side and hugged her mother. "I'm sorry, Mother. I'm sorry," she said softly.

Madeline, crying again, nodded her head. Brenda reached across the table and handed her a napkin. Paul and Ginger's eyes met, and she resumed crying.

It was a heart-tugging moment, a moment that was

awkward on the patio of a crowded restaurant. Most people went about their business. A few people noticed the outpouring of emotion.

"OK," Paul said. "Let's have this toast before people start thinking we're weird or something."

Ginger let her mom go and went back to her seat. But Brenda came over and hugged her. "It's OK to love your daddy and to be emotional about him," Brenda said into her ear. "Trust me, he feels good about it."

"Here we go," Paul said, raising his glass. He was not being disrespectful; he was trying to move beyond it because Madeline got more and more emotional. He recalled attending his grand-mother's funeral and the pastor inciting emotions instead of offering comfort. His posturing seemed contrived. Brenda and Ginger were sincere.

"To Richard Price," Paul said, "a man who remains loved by many and never forgotten."

They tapped glasses and took a sip of the wine. To loosen things, Paul offered an evaluation.

"Next time, I want you to taste it with all your senses," he said. "I want you to put your nose in there good and smell it. Then I want you to twirl it around in your glass to let it oxidize or breathe. Red wine needs to breathe so all its flavors and aromas can come out. Then I want you to lean your glass over and let the wine reach the rim of the glass and then turn it back upright and watch the 'legs,' which is how the residue of the wine goes back to the bottom of the glass. If it's really fast, then the wine is pretty young. But if it flows back slowly, then it's older.

"Then, before you sip it, smell it again—you will notice a difference. It'll be more fragrant. That's what twirling it around does—it brings out the aromas... Now sip it."

The ladies followed his instructions.

"Wow, it does taste better," Madeline said. "It's like all that stuff woke it up."

"That's actually a good way to put it," Paul said.

"It tastes sort of peppery but fruity," Ginger said.

"I can taste the spiciness, too," Brenda said. "Very interesting. I've never paid this much attention to tasting wine before. I sucked it down. If it wasn't bitter, it was OK with me."

"I don't know how or why I was never that way," Paul said. "I, somehow, always appreciated wine."

"I can see a few days with you and Ginger and I'm gonna be a wine snob," Brenda said.

"Well, that's not a bad thing," Paul offered.

They laughed and conversed about the wine, the weather, life and family. Paul excused himself and went to the bathroom. When he returned, he stopped about twenty feet from the table and admired the women—*his* women—laughing and getting along over a glass of wine. And he felt at peace.

CHAPTER 12
THE FAMILY
BUSINESS

Peace can be fleeting, especially among a group of strong-minded people who have strong opinions and are strong debaters whose senses have been heightened by an overconsumption of wine.

And so it was with Paul, Brenda, Madeline and Ginger. They took their lunch love fest to Beringer Winery, where they were impressed with the sheer mass of the facility and the quality of the wines. Paul had looked down on Beringer because it was a "common folk" wine, available in grocery stores.

He was delighted to learn it had excellent, high-quality wines far out of grocery store price points. They sipped on the 2009 Modern Heritage Chardonnay Carneros, the 2010 Modern Heritage Riesling and 2010 Modern Heritage 3 Acre Red Knights Valley.

They then went on to three more wines from the Beringer Private Reserve Cabernet Sauvignons 1996, 2003 and 2006. After tasting a half-dozen wines, the ladies were good and tipsy. Paul felt the effects, too, but he was more himself than the others.

"How we going to another tasting?" Brenda said. "I don't think I can drink anything else right now."

"As much as I'd like to have some more, maybe we should sit down for a while," Madeline said. "After last night, I definitely don't want to push it."

Paul was a little disappointed; he was ready to move on to the next spot, St. Supery Winery. He had a glass of its 2009 Chardonnay at The Lamb's Club during a bus trip to New York the previous summer and loved it so much he tracked it down on winenthusiast.com and located it at Savi market in Atlanta.

He told the ladies they could remain in the tasting room as he went to the Beringer store to order a case to have shipped home. Ginger said, "I want to go." She approached Paul, who whispered to her: "They're buzzing right now. We might not want to leave them alone."

Ginger agreed and went back to sit with the parents. Paul made his way and ordered a case of a combination of the Beringer Reserve wines that totaled more than twelve hundred dollars. That's why he did not want Ginger with him in the wine store—she would have serious questions and demanded answers about him ordering wine that expensive.

He shopped around the expansive store, looking at wine accessories and finally decided he would rejoin the ladies and take them into downtown Napa to shop and see the landscape. But as he approached, he saw expressions on their faces that were not pleasant.

Paul picked up his pace. "How's it going?" he said in a cheerful way when he arrived at the table. But no one else was cheery. "What's going on?"

"We're fine," Ginger said, but they weren't.

"What's going on?" Paul asked again.

"Helena," Ginger said.

"What? What about her?" Paul asked with concern in his voice.

"Your daughter is fine," Brenda said. "But we were arguing—no, discussing—whether you should tell her that she is adopted."

Paul sat down. That was a major point of contention between him and Ginger. He did not want to tell her. Ginger did. Their child was eighteen and totally unaware that her parents were not her biological parents.

"How did you all get on this subject?" Paul said.

"She texted me a photo of her and her friend and I showed them the photo," Ginger said.

"Yeah, she texted me the same photo," Paul said. "And…"

"And I said it's remarkable that she looks like Ginger even though she's not her mother," Brenda said.

"Ma, what do you mean?" Paul said, his nose flaring open.

"That's what I'm talking about," Ginger said.

"I didn't mean it that way," Brenda said.

"Ginger is the only mother Helena will ever know, so for you to say that is so insulting," Madeline said.

Their happy family had deteriorated in the time it took Paul to purchase a case of wine.

"Ginger, I am sorry; I really didn't mean it that way," Brenda said. "You're that child's mother and you've been a great mother, too. That's why she's such a fine young lady, because of you and Paul. I'm sorry. I was not trying to disrespect you. Why would I?"

"Well, thank you for saying that, Miss Wall. I am very sensitive around this subject. That girl feels like she came out of my stomach," Ginger said.

"And that's why we don't have to tell her about her biological parents," Paul said. "She's as much a part of you as if she came out of you."

"But that's not right," Madeline said. "She should know where she comes from. She should understand her history."

"That's right, Mother," Ginger contributed.

"But even if that history is not going to make her feel good?" Brenda said.

"It's not a pretty history," Paul said, "and I don't want my baby thinking anything less of herself because of the sperm donors' horrible lives."

The divide and animosity was palpable: mother and son felt one way; daughter and mother felt another. And as sweet and wonderful as it felt at the restaurant, it was that sour and antagonistic at the winery.

They sat at the table in the tasting room, which had all but emptied, and had a knockdown drag-out. Paul and Brenda's position was based on the knowledge that the natural parents of Helena were criminals who would not see freedom for another five years. The mother, in fact, gave birth with one arm handcuffed to a hospital bed.

A week from delivering a child, she and her co-criminal boyfriend robbed a gas station convenience store and were caught after an extended high-speed chase. They shot the worker, although he gave up the money without hesitation. The pregnant mother was the driver of the getaway car police followed for miles through Atlanta traffic before finally being cornered, ironically enough, on Freedom Parkway.

There was a shootout for several minutes or until they ran out of bullets. It was then that they surrendered. Had the television cameras not been present, they likely would have gotten shot, despite giving up.

Two days later, Helena was born—in the Atlanta Federal Penitentiary hospital. The mother got a day to recover and was back in her cell where she faced multiple counts of armed robbery, attempted murder of a police officer (because of a shootout with authorities) and possession of an unregistered gun and stolen goods, among other charges.

The father was in prison on the same charges when the baby was born. They were a criminal team that worked in tandem wreaking havoc for years, robbing people, assaulting people and generally being a menace to society.

They both expressed no interest in even seeing the baby. And because their families' lives were just as troubled, there was no one to turn the baby over to if they wanted; no one who could do the child good, that is. Even in their psychosis of committing crimes, they understood the best option for the child was to put her up for adoption.

"Take it out of me and give it a chance to do some good," the woman said before going into labor. "I don't deserve nobody to call me 'Momma.' What can I do for a baby? If I wasn't going to jail, what can I teach a child? How to be a criminal? That's what happened to me. I might have messed up my life, but I ain't trying to create another me. I know enough to recognize that's wrong."

"And you want me to tell my daughter that's where she comes from?" Paul said. "That's not fair to her. It would be one thing if they said, 'Let me at least see the baby. Let me hold her.' They said the opposite. So if they don't want to know the baby at all, why should we put her in that crazy world that they come from? It could make her look at herself in some kind of crazy way. I think she's fragile enough to be affected by it."

Ginger saw it differently. "That's so wrong, Paul," she said. "We all should know where we come from. And although we raised her from her first days on this earth, she has natural parents that she should know about. And knowing about them shouldn't break her or make her look at herself in some strange way; we raised her to be strong and independent.

"It would be very selfish to prevent her from knowing this truth, Paul. That's not how it should be."

"And," Madeline contributed, "I was a nurse for thirty years. The fact that you all do not know her family's health history is not good. So many health issues and conditions are handed down through bloodlines. Heart disease. Diabetes. You just don't know. And even mental health issues. If her parents were both doing criminal things, there could be a gene that triggers such behavior. All this is very important."

"Haven't you all been on top of her visiting the doctor and taking all sorts of tests?" Brenda asked. "You've done your part. You think you're going to get the information you need from that family about family history? It's as dysfunctional as it gets. I don't have to tell you this. You did the research. You knew from the beginning that they would be in prison and they wouldn't be the kind of people you'd want Helena associated with. So why now, when she's in college and her life is great? All it's going to do is upset her. No good will come out of it."

They had asked for a bottle of Cab while Paul was in the bathroom, and it arrived just before Ginger was to add to her argument. The server wanted to pour the wine, but Paul told her, "I got it. Thanks," so she went on and they went on.

"Nothing bad will come out of it, either," Ginger said. "I…"

She went silent. "I don't feel so good; a little queasy," she said.

"No more wine for you for a while," Paul said, handing her a glass of water.

"You OK, Ginger?" her mom asked.

After a few sips of water, she sat back in her seat.

"This argument is making me sick," she said. "Paul, Miss Wall, what if Helena finds out about her parents from some other source? What if they are rehabilitated while in prison and in a few years—they are eligible to be released in five years—and they decide they want to at least meet the child they created? And they find us and approach Helena. You've seen the movies and how that turns out; it's ugly.

"I have never seen or even heard of a case where a kid is not upset when he finds out that his parents did not tell him about his birth parents. There is a natural interest to know where you come from, whether it's good or bad."

"I don't know about that," Paul said. "I wouldn't want to know that my parents were criminals. That wouldn't make me feel good."

"But would it make you feel good," Madeline interjected, "to learn that your parents who raised you made a decision to be dishonest with you about something really important?"

"Well, who says she has to know?" Brenda jumped in. "Who's going to tell her?"

"Brenda, that's not the right approach," Madeline said. "We can't have something like this hanging over her, over the families."

"It's been like this for eighteen years and I don't feel bothered by it," Paul said. "And Helena is living her life, having a great time. It's not hanging over her, either."

Paul sipped his wine and it began to settle in. He felt a little lightheaded, which intensified his emotions.

Ginger stared at her husband from across the table. It was not an angry or a comforting look. It was as if she could see what was in his heart.

"You're scared," she said to Paul, who swirled his wine as if he did not hear Ginger. "Look at me, Paul. You're scared."

"Scared?" Paul said, looking confused. "Scared of what?"

"Scared that your baby will look at you differently," Ginger said.

Paul just looked at her.

"Paul, honey, don't you know nothing could change who you are to her?" Ginger said. "You are the apple of her eye, and vice-versa. She's a daddy's girl. You're a girl's daddy. No one comes before you."

Paul's eyes began to water. Alcohol increased his emotions.

"You took her to her doctor's appointments when she was a baby," Ginger went on. "You taught her how to ride a bike and how to drive a car and everything in between: basketball, golf and cards and even how to get what she wanted out of me.

"When I dropped her off at college, we both cried in the room. I said, 'Why are you crying?' She said, ''Cause I miss Daddy already.' You and I have had our issues, yes. But that is your daughter. She loves you more than anyone in the world. You've got to know that."

Tears rolled down Paul's face, and he did not even bother to wipe them.

Brenda put her arm around her son. "Is that it, Vino?"

she said in a comforting voice. "Is that what you think? Oh, no, son. You can't lose that girl. You're everything to her."

She treated him as if he were a three-year-old, wiping his face clear of tears. He just shook his head.

"It's OK," Brenda said.

"I just… We just put so much of ourselves into her," Paul said. "I don't want anything to take away from that."

"But nothing can, Paul," Brenda said. "Because we've put so much into her we must be honest with her on this. Remember when she was a tiny baby and we sat in the living room, on the couch, and you held her in your arms and you looked at me and said, 'She deserves us and we deserve this little angel.'"

"I do remember that," Paul said. "I'm shocked you remember it. That was eighteen years ago."

"I remember it because it was important," Ginger said. "You said she deserves us because you knew we would never let her down and teach her and mold her and protect her and be there for her. She deserved that. Well, she also deserves to know about her parents. To not tell her would not be protecting her. It would be letting her down."

And those were the words that turned Paul—and his mother. The idea of letting down Helena did not compute with him. It was not an option. He lavished her with love and attention—and all the latest technological gadgets, too—but mostly with love. The fact that he considered breaking up his family spoke to how jumbled his mind and self-esteem were at the time.

"You're right," Paul said. "It would be letting her down—and not believing in the bond we have—to keep it from her. So, how do we tell her something so delicate? When do we do it?"

"Should have already been done," Madeline said. "I thought four years ago, when she went to high school was the time. But…"

"Well, we can't go back in time," Brenda said.

"She's coming home for Christmas," Paul said. "That gives us about a month to figure out how to tell her."

"Drink plenty of wine," Brenda said. "It will help the truth come out."

They laughed, finally, and lifted their glasses.

"To Helena," Paul said. "My daughter. *Our* daughter." And they tapped glasses and drank of the wine.

CHAPTER 13
AND THE PLOTS THICKEN

Because Madeline and Brenda were afraid to drink more, considering how the previous night ended, and with Ginger complaining of a queasy stomach and lightheadedness, the group decided to go back to the hotel after the discussion.

"How about I order some appetizers and we sit by the pool and relax?" Paul suggested. "There is still some sunlight left in the day."

Ginger pulled Paul aside. "So you just insist on spending all your money?" she said.

"No, that's not it," Paul answered. "I want to maximize this trip, this place. It's beautiful out here."

"Don't you think maybe we should talk some more about Helena?"

"OK," Paul said. "I thought we were done. Can we do it out here? It's a nice day to sit outside and talk."

"Fine," Ginger said.

Madeline and Brenda told their children they would connect with them for dinner. "This was a really nice day, Paul," Madeline said. "I enjoyed all of it."

"Me, too," Brenda interjected. "Looking forward to a

nice dinner—after I get a nap. Between last night and the wine tasting, I need to rejuvenate."

And off they went. Paul grabbed Ginger's hand and led her to the pool area, where he ordered a glass of Viognier. Ginger passed.

"The truth of the matter is I have something that needs to be said," she started. "I don't know if it's the wine or if it's my conscience. It's probably more the wine because I haven't felt the need to say this when I'm totally sober."

She looked around to see if anyone was near; they were the only guests by the rectangular-shaped pool. The sun was brilliant, so much so that Ginger dug through her purse to pull out a pair of sunglasses. She had Paul's in there, too, and handed him his.

"What's wrong, Gin?" Paul wanted to know. "It's OK. I agree with you and your mother. Let's tell Heather about her natural parents. I'm OK with it."

"I'm glad you are," she said. "But that's not it. Well, that's not totally it. Talking about it today, telling you that she deserved to know it and that we owed her the truth, made me realized I owe you the truth, too."

Paul's thoughts were all over the place. Was she speaking of his firing because of the sexual harassment complaint? Had that woman contacted her? He met a woman at Whole Foods one day, got her phone number but never called when the woman indicated she worked at the same building as Ginger. Could she have said something to his wife? Did she know about him winning the lottery? *How could she*, he thought. He only told Big Al, and he knew Big Al was as trustworthy as could be.

He pondered all those possibilities as quickly as he could to come up with an answer that might minimize the presumed trouble he was in. But Ginger wanted to speak of something else.

"I must preface this by saying that there was a period several months ago where we were over in my mind," she began. "And if the wine didn't have me buzzing, I probably wouldn't even say anything now. Anyway, you told me you wanted a divorce and that you didn't want me anymore. And—"

"I've apologized about this time and time again," Paul said. "And I will continue to apologize about it. I wasn't in my right mind. You've known me for more than twenty years. That was like someone other than me was speaking. I was in a bad place. But that's part of why we're here, to get beyond that."

"I know," Ginger said. "But this is something else. Please, let me get it out. I think it's the reason why I was so upset that day I told you I was all panicked in the garage. It was more than having to live with you without Helena there as a buffer. It was living with myself, what I did, that was also bothering me."

Paul's mind immediately switched to infidelity. What else could it be that she would have trouble living with herself? And in an instant he was mad, furious, embarrassed, humiliated, jealous. It is with that speed a man can get to all those emotions when he believes his woman has betrayed him.

"What did you do, Ginger?" he said. He needed to hear the words. Not that they would be soothing. "What did you do?"

The server arrived with his glass of wine and Paul did not bother to even acknowledge her. "Ginger," he repeated, "what did you do?"

She looked into his eyes, eyes that were far from comforting. "Paul, after you told me you wanted a divorce, I was lost and hurt and didn't know what to do with my life," she began. "In that moment, I realized that my life was hinged on our marriage. I sunk everything into you and Helena and now it was falling apart. I didn't know what to do."

Paul sat with his arms folded, waiting for the real news.

"The day before you told me you wanted a divorce, I learned I was pregnant," Ginger added. Paul unfolded his arms and sat up in his chair.

"What?" he said, amazement all over his face. "I thought, I mean…the doctors said…you know…"

"I know; they said I couldn't get pregnant," Ginger stepped in. "We tried for years but nothing happened. Well, that one time when we basically just needed to be physical with each other—we were in the middle of all our drama—produced a pregnancy."

Paul was relieved, shocked and delighted.

"Are you telling me we have a baby coming?" he said, smiling while looking down at her stomach.

His response made the news Ginger had to share even more devastating.

"No, Paul, we don't," she answered softly.

"But you said you were…" His voice drifted off as the realization of what happened hit him.

"I had an abortion, Paul," she managed to get out.

Paul literally shook his head, as if the words would be jumbled and came out to mean something else. But there was no mistaking what she said.

"You had an abortion? What are you talking about?" Paul said, sounding confused.

"You told me you wanted a divorce," Ginger said. "You said you didn't want me anymore. What was I to do? Bring a child into a world where we were going to split up? It seemed crazy to me at the time. I don't hate anyone, but I truly detested you. You were mean and cold and totally dismissive of me, as if I was some rag doll."

"Still, Ginger, you don't get rid of a baby without talking to your husband," Paul said. He noticed his voice rose and looked around to see if anyone was there to hear. There was not.

"We weren't talking at all, Paul," she said, tears forming in her eyes. "What was I supposed to do? You didn't want me. That's what you told me. How could I think you'd want a baby?"

Paul shook his head. He never expressed to Ginger

how much he always wanted a child born of his genes. Instead, at the time, he comforted Ginger when the doctors told her she could not conceive. He loved Helena as if she were of his body. But if they could have had a child between them, it would have meant everything to him.

"An abortion?" Paul said. "I know we weren't talking. I know what I said. But, still. That's a pretty big deal, Ginger. You...Didn't you know how much I wanted a child with you?"

"No," she said. "The next day after the pregnancy test came back positive—you didn't even notice that I was sick and sluggish—you came home and told me you didn't want me anymore. That's what I remember. And I knew then what I had to do.

"It was the hardest decision of my life. I wanted a baby so badly, too. But I wanted a family more. And if I couldn't have a family with you, it didn't make sense to have a baby...I was devastated when I couldn't have a child and I was shocked when I was pregnant. It told me the doctors do not have power over God. I was so happy.

"Why do you think I cooked that nice meal that night? We hadn't been talking or anything. But I had a nice meal and sat there with you at the table. That was the night I was going to tell you, hoping that the news would bring you around, make you see we had something to bring us back together. And before I can say anything, you tell me you want a divorce. I was livid and hurt and, to be honest, devastated. But mostly, I was confused. There was nothing to say after you so coldly told me what you wanted."

"Oh, my God," Paul said. "You might not understand it, but that was an unselfish act I was trying to make that night. I was basically saying you deserve better than me. I wasn't being the man I needed to be for you. I was at a low point and I didn't see any way to come out of it. The way I lost my job, which you didn't even know about. The terrible job market. Doing the odd jobs to keep food on the table. I felt like I was dissolving into nothing. You deserved more."

His voice drifted off. Ginger wiped her face and reached over to hold Paul's hand. He pulled it away.

"But you took the one thing away from me that could have changed my life," he said, the anger in his voice distinctive. "You knew how much a child would have meant to me. We talked about it for years. Helena brought us the best joy we could have received. But she also was a blessing because we loved her so much we stopped talking about not being able to have a child. And now, you somehow get pregnant—a miracle—and you kill the baby? How could you do that?"

"Paul, that's a very mean thing to say, way to put it," she said. "I didn't know what to do. I was confused. I—"

"That's when you talk to your husband, dammit," Paul said. "You don't go off and get rid of a baby without talking to your husband. I don't care what I said to you that night. What you did was bigger than what I said."

Ginger's emotions ran high, but she remained poised. "You've got to know that was not an easy decision for me," she said. "But I had to do what I thought was right. I have beaten myself up about it every day since then. But I'm not going to let you beat me up, too. If you had been more of a man and faced your challenges instead of giving in to them, we wouldn't even be here. That's the hard truth and I'm sorry I am saying it to you like this. But it's the truth. So, you can blame me all you want—and I understand why you would—but you know the truth."

"Oh, so it's my fault that you went out and did what you did?" Paul said.

"It's my body and my life," Ginger said, getting angry. "I'm not going to let you make me feel more upset about it than I have already been. But until the last several weeks, I didn't feel that badly. I felt like I did the right thing. You weren't fit to be a father to a baby. You were acting like a baby yourself."

"Kiss my ass, Ginger," Paul said, rising from the table. He turned to walk away, but turned back to pick up his glass of wine off the table and stormed off, leaving his wife there with her thoughts.

She was so angry she could not even cry. He made her question her decision, but she believed she did the right thing at the time. Still, his words could not be ignored. Maybe her decision was hasty. Maybe she should have thought about how the news of her pregnancy would positively influence Paul. Maybe she should have taken her friend Serena's advice, which was to consult with Paul. But she did not want him to want the marriage for a baby; she wanted him to want *her*. But her struggle with the decision from that moment on was an indicator of knowing she was not happy with her decision.

Ginger decided she would find Paul and let him know how she felt. But when she got to the room, he was not there. She called him on his cell phone, but it rang in their room; he left it there. She was frustrated, and went to the parking lot to see if the rental car was still there. It wasn't.

Paul had taken his drink and his anger and his pain to the car. He started driving with no destination in mind. He needed to get away, to clear his head, to figure out his feelings. The disappointment in Ginger did not diminish his feelings for her. But it did upset him in a way he could not articulate or even identify. His mind took him to several dark places—Ginger going under the knife to have the abortion; what the child would have looked like; and even his role in her decision. Paul was a mental wreck.

He ended up on in the northern block of Napa's downtown district at 1313 Main, a swanky wine bar that had a warm and inviting feel. That was exactly what he needed.

Paul was lucky to get a small corner table on the lovely patio that was fenced in by lush greenery. After nearly fifteen minutes of contemplation, he ordered a bottle of Caymus 2008 Cabernet Sauvignon. It cost $163. He did not care. He wanted to lose himself in the wine.

He did not bother to ask his server about the wine. He wanted to test his senses. He looked around at the mass of people smiling and enjoying each other and it saddened him. He learned some-thing about his wife that he thought it was best he did not know: That she had the capacity to deceive him.

Never mind that he kept the truth from her about why he lost his job. That did not come into his mind. He could only see what was in front of him, and that was that he had a chance to father a child and Ginger took it from him.

When the wine came, he had to shake himself of his thoughts. The Caymus was a lush wine, rich in color and flavor. He inhaled it deeply to let the aroma rise through his nostrils. He closed his eyes to appreciate it.

He then set it on the table and placed the stem of the glass between his index and third fingers and began slowly swirling it around, to help the wine breathe and to release all of its flavors. After a minute or so of that action, he smelled it again, and this time the aromas seemed to burst into the air, causing a small smile to crease his face.

He was having the best time—and he hadn't even tasted the wine yet.

He swirled it some more and finally, deliberately moved

the glass toward his mouth. It was a delicate and careful maneuver, as if he were placing one of Ginger's breasts in his mouth. When he finally creased his lips to place the rim of the glass between them, he took in another deep smell of the wine, and he was almost mesmerized by it.

The wine funneled into his mouth and he let it wade there so his tongue could consume it all. He detected a complex mix of dark fruit, blackberry and plum with a hint of licorice and spices. It was a full-bodied wine, one that had a strong finish but no aftertaste.

Paul was in love.

It was the best wine he had ever consumed, and he treated it as such, pampering it and seducing it as he ingested it. It was so good and fulfilling that for a time, he did not even think about Ginger and the mess he considered his life to be.

By the fourth glass, he was officially on buzz—and the reality of his life came back to him. He wished Ginger had kept that secret to herself. Knowing it confused him. Part of him despised that she made such a major decision without his input; another part of him admired her honesty. Those conflicting emotions and the wine clashed to make his head spin.

One moment he thought of calling her to talk it out, but it was then that he realized he left his cell phone in the room. The next moment he actually pondered getting a hotel room and staying away for the night as a way of clearing his head. The truth was that it would be a way of punishing her, and, as mad and disappointed as he was, he couldn't bring himself to torture his wife.

As he finished the last glass, he wondered what Ginger was doing, how she was feeling about him not being accessible. He was always in reach of her. To be as disconnected as he was at this time with the issue hanging over them had to be driving her crazy, he thought. And he did gain a little pleasure out of that, but not so much that he would allow it to linger much longer.

He enjoyed the last sip, paid for the bottle with his debit card and headed to the car to go back to the hotel and face the issue that was impossible to ignore and likely would take quite a while to overcome. Before leaving, his server asked if he would like a glass of water; he could sense Paul's equilibrium was off.

"I can't put water on top of a wine like that," Paul said. "Thank you, though."

And he made his way to the rental car and started back to the hotel, well enough, considering his thoughts were all over the place and that he was drunk. He did not know if he could ever forgive Ginger for aborting his child, and that scared him because he loved her. He was anxious to talk it out with her to see if he could arrive at a different emotion.

However, when he reached the second light on Main Street, he stopped in the middle of the intersection. He was not sure why. He thought the light turned red and